EL NIÑO

stories by

Sharon Doubiago

EL NIÑO

Lost Roads Number 35 1989

Library of Congress Cataloging in Publication Data
Doubiago, Sharon El Niño
(Lost Roads series; no. 35)
I. Title
PS3554.0814N56 1988 813'.54 88-13787
ISBN 0-918786-39-8

P.O. Box 5848 Weybosset Hill Station
Providence, Rhode Island
First Printing by McNaughton & Gunn
Typeset by The Writer's Center, Bethesda, Maryland

Cover photograph "No One's Angel" by Kay Duvernet
Book design by C.D. Wright and Forrest Gander

This project is supported by a grant from the National Endowment for the Arts in Washington, D.C., a federal agency.

ALSO FROM LOST ROADS

Poetry

Ralph Adamo, *Sadness at the Private University; The End of the World*
Irv Broughton, *The Blessing of the Fleet*
Justin Caldwell, *The Sleeping Porch*
Mark Craver, *The Problem of Grace*
Quinton Duval, *Dinner Music*
Phillip Foss, *The Compisition of Glass*
Fanny Howe, *The Vineyard*
Honor Johnson, *Small As a Resurrection*
Frances Mayes, *Hours*
John McKernan, *Walking Along the Missouri River*
John S. Morris, *Bean Street*
Stan Rice, *Body of Work*
Frank Stanford, *The Singing Knives; You; The Battlefield Where the Moon Says I Love You*
Arthur Sze, *River, River*
Carolyn Beard Whitlow, *Wild Meat*

Fiction

Alison Bundy, *A Bad Business*
Mary Caponegro, *Tales from the Next Village*
Myra Sklarew, *Like a Field Riddled By Ants*
Steve Stern, *Isaac and the Undertaker's Daughter*

In Translation

René Char, No Siege is Absolute versions by Franz Wright
Philippe Soupault, *I'm Lying* translated by Paulette Schmidt

Art

Zuleyka Benitez, *Trouble in Paradise*

Travel

Barbara and Sandra Heller, New Orleans My Darling

Also by Sharon Doubiago

Poetry

Hard Country (West End Press, 1982)
South America Mi Hija (Calyx, 1989)
Oedipus Drowned (Pygmy Forest, 1988)
Psyche Drive The Coast, poems 1975-1987 (Empty Bowl, 1989)

Stories

The Book Of Seeing With One's Own Eyes (Graywolf, 1988)

for el niño
in weather and flesh

El Niño is a warm water wind that originates at Christmas time off the coast of Peru. It is named The Boy for the child whose birth is celebrated then.

Since 1940, there have been ten El Niños. The last three—in 1976-77, 1982-83 and 1986-87—have been strong enough to affect the weather, but not in the same way. The 1982-83 pattern brought extremely high precipitation to the Northwest. The 1976-77 and 1986-87 patterns brought droughts.

The Oregonian, November 1, 1987

Grateful acknowledgement is made to the following publications in which earlier versions of some of these stories first appeared:

"Lulu in Brazil": River Styx (1983), *The Sun* (Santa Cruz, California, 1986)

"Navarro Bluff": *Arts and Entertainment Magazine* (The Mendocino Art Center, 1978) and *California Living Magazine* (The Chronicle, 1978)

"Life In The Great Northwest Somewhere": *Arts and Entertainment Magazine* (Mendocino Art Center, 1984)

The author wishes to express her gratitude to the Ucross Foundation, the Montalvo Association, the Wolfpen Writers Colony, and the Djerassi Foundation for their generous hospitality.

TABLE

I.
Moonlight and Roses Remind Me Of You

BEAUTY AND THE BEAST

Can that be Love, that drinks another as a sponge drinks water?
William Blake

The man sits down beside us smelling of alcohol and the vomit that is splashed down the front of his shirt. He cranes his neck to me, staring, while we try to watch the film, *Beauty and the Beast*, in this small theater in New Hampshire. All through the movie he stares at me as if I am the movie, as if my nine year old daughter and my twelve year old son are not sitting in the seats on the other side of me.

my heart is good but I am
a beast.
You cannot
love me.
So do it again,
reject me
that I may retreat
still further
into my pure heart,
drown in its tears
away away from this
beastly flesh
and your beauty
which is ugly
which causes
my pain
my ugliness

◇ ◇ ◇

Lizard loved me in high school. I dated him every other weekend for years because that was the only way my father, somehow wise in the folly of total prohibition, would allow me to see, on alternate weekends, the Indian boy I loved.

He said he fell in love with me on the summer before his junior year when he was leaning against the corner of the Rexall Drugstore on Main Street watching me come up the street on my way to Angel Park swimming pool. I had just turned thirteen. When I came even with him he said I looked into his eyes, smiled, and said hello.

No one had ever smiled at me before. No one in this town ever said hello to me.

He had lived in Ramona since he was five when his mother left his father in New Hampshire and came to the place near her sister who lived with the Indians.

All my friends pitied me, forced by my father to go with the creepiest guy in school, in order to see my real love. Our dates were usually to the movies at the Ramona Theatre. During intermission he would buy me double decker ice cream cones from El Patio next door, something my parents could never afford. I don't know how Lizard afforded them. He would come down from the high school to the junior high at recess and lunch and mope around, watch me from the baseball stands as I made-out under them with Ramon. Or when Ramon was missing, lost in the hills, the sheriff looking for him, follow me as I wandered around awkwardly in the dust, not knowing what to do with myself. He always followed at a distance so I couldn't protest, at least that's what I thought, his hunched silhouette against the blinding sun so often there, one I learned to ignore, perhaps accept. I felt sorry for him. During the summer he was at the swimming pool every day when I swam, swam and paid no attention to him. I only *had* to pay attention to him every other Saturday.

But he was the only boy welcomed at our house on Olive Street Hill and he took full advantage of this. He was there nearly every night that first year when we were trying to figure a way to make a living in the town. He was hard to ignore then. My father was still commuting, first to Los Angeles, then to San Diego, to the aircraft plants. Lizard teased us about the fact that we ate so much hamburger. Three hundred and sixty five ways to prepare cow, he'd say. It was Lizard's idea that we open a hamburger stand.

When I was in the eighth grade he gave me a pair of shoes that were the latest, *white bunny ears*. It was a strange, rather wonderful gift, one I never could have afforded myself. My mother said it was wrong for men to give women clothes. If you accepted such an intimate gift it meant you had no self-respect. But a pair of shoes didn't seem intimate to me and finally she relented, probably for the same reason my father insisted on the relationship, hoping to draw me from Ramon. They didn't seem to consider how little respect this boy could have for himself, or that I could have for him as the pawn in their schemes. The shoes, with their rabbit ears sticking up the back of my bare ankles, were a size too small and in six months I had a painful growth on one of my toes that required surgery and several weeks of therapy with the podiatrist in Escondido, the larger town twenty miles below Ramona. When, upon examining me this doctor wanted to break all the bones in my legs and feet, put me in casts for two years so that I would walk "correctly," I said no. He may have been the first man planning to remake me in his image of perfection that I said no to.

The first time I went into Ramona High School was with Lizard. Most of the Indian guys and the whites who hung out with them had animal names: Fish, Snake, Buzzard, Coyote, Porky, Tarantula, Rooster. In the main hallway, in the Angel Hall of Fame cabinet, a photograph of Lizard's cousin was on display, a basketball star who years ago had died of a heart attack during a championship play-off game. The picture showed him shooting a free-throw and his name was Horse, even back then, though he was white, "the only white relative besides my mother I got in this town." Now Lizard had made the basketball team which was confusing for everyone because, as he said, "no one can stand me." He said he fell in love with me when I told him that I prayed he would win a trophy. No one has ever cared for me before. He said that many times. And then he won a trophy.

When he graduated from high school the year I entered high school he became one of those few who stayed in the town, wearing his humiliation like scaley skin, like vestigial limbs I suppose you could say since his name was Lizard. Anyone with any self-respect left Ramona immediately but Lizard said he loved Ramona. He said he couldn't leave because of me.

Cold winter nights with snow on Palomar Mountain twenty miles above us, he hung around the drive-in stand my father designed and built of redwood, drinking in the bushes with the Indians, tottering back when I came on shift, sometimes bringing me a rose from the alley, and we would talk through the hand-out windows till closing, midnight, rock n roll from the jukebox, *you ain't nothin but a hound dog!* the loud cars and neon lights of the small mountain town racing behind this poor soul hanging aroumd me for years, the first guy I ever really talked to.

I never realized, I guess because the relationship carried the onus of force and because my mother had warned me for years that if you were friendly to guys they would get the wrong idea, that in a strange way Lizard became a close friend. He teased me a lot as I made and wrapped and served hamburgers, french fries, and malts, carried on my painfully tongue-tied, newly developing waitress banter with everyone who came to the windows. He said I was right not to let the doctor break my legs, I walked in a sexy way. He said his aunt who lived with the Indians knew real medicine, healing powers in rocks and weeds and that doctor just wanted to hook us for the money. He called me *Blondie* and batted around the name *El Angel's Heavenly Hamburgers.* Customers, especially strangers, always called me Blondie, but I think it was through Lizard that I began to know something about the power and meaning in words, in my own names. We talked those drive-in nights about everything, analyzing the people of our town and country—gossip and politics and religions, Indians and the worth of rock and roll and the meaning of life—evolving a real relationship out of the false construct of my father. When my father told me recently that these days, so many years later, Lizard has a poetry manuscript a foot thick I was at first astonished—ours was not a town to produce one poet, much less two—but then I remember, more in my body than in my mind, how our conversations verged on the creative, on the play and concern with words and ideas and what was happening to the world, and the expression returns rather gently that I once heard from a professor that filled me then with loathing, shame and rage: *redneck intellectuals*.

The only thing Lizard and I didn't talk about was Sergei, the boy I fell in love with after Ramon, the sailor I planned to marry as soon as I graduated, the boy who would be the father of my children. I knew he knew about Sergei. Everyone in Ramona knew about Sergei. My father's conditional prohibition in regards to Ramon had turned unconditional with Sergei: I was forbidden to ever see him.

Sometimes Lizard's mother came to the window, a small intense black-haired woman with a chiseled face like his, except she was pretty. We never acknowledged the person we shared, her son who was becoming a sort of mirror for me. He was a boy; I was a girl. He was old; I was young. He was dumb; I was smart. He was wasting his life; mine was before me. He was ugly; I was beautiful. Everyone said these things. I studied his face framed in the aluminum service window until I found myself seeing through his ugly mask, seeing interesting lines, the jaw and lips and nose and eyes of his mother, the thick black curls over the granite face. He looked like the mime in that other movie I've never been able to forget, *The Children of Paradise*, the lithe athlete's body as he walked away under the street lamps of Main Street at closing, so surprisingly, despite its slouch, its depression, full of grace and rhythm and story.

Though he had graduated from high school and graduates were

forbidden he always managed to get into El Angel Hall where we had our Friday night dances, the quonset hut that had once been a real bar and still, unmistakably, carried the aura, out in the eucalyptus grove on Highway 67 just before the long mountain descent to San Diego and the sea, the long dangerous mountain road on which our friends—first Porky, then Coyote—were already dying. Today that road is called Slaughter Alley.

And this was when I would really get beyond his ugly face and this was always confusing, my friends snickering as he teeters heavy-limbed across the room to ask me to dance and I pretend I share their disgust for there is no way to tell them the strange thing, that when this creep takes me in his arms and I can no longer see him, the stench of alcohol and body odor sending me reeling and he begins reeling me across the dark floor, through and around the other reeling bodies, the music drinking us deeper into the reservation's bass and bang and piano wail on the floor, till he is sobbing in my ear, against my neck, his convulsions some of the first in the dark familiar rhythm I will pursue all my life, the coming, the crying, the birthings, the dyings, the beat of the blood through the organs of our bodies and I begin to understand the deal my father has made with me, for just as in the movie the hall is filled with a blaze of light and the mirror shatters and I see in the thousand pieces on the floor that I too am the beautiful awful beast.

The week before I was married, one week after I graduated from high school, Lizard trapped me in my car after I closed the drive-in at midnight. He grabbed my keys and said I couldn't go until I gave him a kiss. Just one kiss to remember the rest of his life. His week old beard was caked with booze, dried egg yolk and vomit.

"Lizard, I can't. I'm getting married Friday."

I had to be true to Sergei. I couldn't begin my marriage with an infidelity and a confession and the shadow that would cast over it. To stay true to my fiance I had just come through the most painful two years of my life—forbidden to see him, the whole town against us, the disciplines of my father, the tempting seductions of time and other men. I had even controlled the great physical passions of my body during our secret rendezvous. I had kept my vow to remain a virgin for my husband. There was no way I was going to be untrue now.

At first he was firm in his resolve, but as the hour passed he began to beg, then cry, then scream. I pleaded with him, caught in the saliva strung between his upper and lower teeth, as I had for years with my father, to understand, understand *me*, see yourself, you're setting yourself up, it's not me that's the problem. He tilted his head back, sucked on his bottle. I could see myself in his watery eyes. Something hung from his nose, oh Lizard, don't you ever look in the mirror? The eucalyptus swayed above us across the moon. He wouldn't let me go. The same old movie, all the future all the past, will I ever get free of this town? his hands like claws grabbing me, like grips slinging me, like Daddy's forcing me.

The garbage bins we were parked up against stank, *Angel's* in my father's hand across the cinder blocks. I'd been on my feet eight hours making hamburgers, and before that, since dawn, sewing my wedding dress. I wanted to go to sleep, his arm across the top of the blue plastic seat. I shut my eyes, saw Sergei, saw myself coming down the aisle to him, then driving far away from Ramona. Little could I imagine what my wedding night would actually bring, but if I had kissed Lizard I would have always thought that's what jinxed us. The minutes passed as red pepper seeds dropping one at a time on the roof and hood of my baby blue 53 Ford, the car I'd worked so long and hard for. Then his fingers were around my neck and he was raging again.

In the fairy tale the girl with heart kisses the monster. I was a girl with heart. But I couldn't force my lips to Lizard's. So much of the relationship with him had been forced. It felt as if to kiss him would destroy the heart between us, would bind us tighter to the same old plot. It's you Lizard who needs more heart. You yank my hair, force my head back, my mouth up to yours, as if it's my fault. Force my lips to yours and you will be saved. My Prince in disguise. But *we* will be lost, I know it! Now you lay yourself down in my lap like a baby I'm to take care of. Am I cruel as you cry? What can a little kiss matter? I don't need to tell Sergei. Photos of those six year old brides and grooms in India floated in the silver dollars of the eucalyptus, the Bible stories of girls forced to marry old men. Why does growing up mean you must go against all your instincts? Sell your soul to the Devil, kiss the Beast, you will see the light, you will be rewarded. They don't want you to know who you really are, what love really is. Will this night ever pass? The Indians sleeping in the alley are moaning from nightmares. I love you Lizard. Maybe I should kiss you. But it's not right. It'd be like rape.

When the sun came up that morning over the valley of granite boulders and the quail began running in coveys across the alley calling their chi-*ca*-go! chi-*ca*-go! one of the places I intended to go in my new life, Lizard let me go. Without a kiss.

My father says you still see Lizard walking down Main Street, dragging himself hunched and defeated from The Turkey Inn to The Crazy Horse Saloon, a balding middle-aged man. And my brother says, shit, you should see him weaving down the highway, swinging his arms like an ape from The Hilltop to The Tepee Room, the alcohol has him so bad one little drink and he goes bananas. When he can work he delivers firewood—at Christmas, mistletoe—from the Laguna Mountains to La Jolla where he has made the acquaintance of Dr. Suess who encourages him in his poetry for children, and you know, it was Lizard who founded the Little League in Ramona. But the alcohol, it's got him bad. Though still, Daddy says, after all these years, he asks about you. Where you are now. Who you're married to now. Heard she's a mother. Heard's she's a hippy. Heard she's a feminist. Heard she's a poet. And sometimes then he starts crying. He says he's a poet too. I don't know what to do then. He had his chances. I just can't understand why he didn't make something of himself. You know—and my father slips then into his oldest stance with me—he says it's your fault.

◇ ◇ ◇

The man beside us continues to stare while on the screen that flickers the oldest shadows across our bodies, Beauty's father, to save himself, offers his daughter to the Beast. He stares at me expectantly, instructing my children, how I'm to solve his problem for him, his putrid smell reeling us up in a dark medieval dance. When finally I turn and look into his face the same question rises in me that has always risen in me. What is a face? I am watching Cocteau's *Beauty and the Beast* with my son and daughter in a dark winter hall in New Hampshire, a state where in so many faces I see the old face of my great secret friend, Lizard. It is said there are human beings beneath the masks of men and women. It is said the meaning of this fairy tale from the Old World is that men know, and love their bestialness, their evil as well as their good, that women must submit to this evil in order to learn compassion. But the deepest meaning is to reinforce the Father's rule, to corrupt the Child, to bring us under the authority of the State. *"A creeping skeleton with lamplike eyes watching around a frozen marriage bed."* Beauty inside the boy must be betrayed. Beast inside the girl must be betrayed. Lizard, you taught me this, once upon a time long ago in a town furthest west, named for a girl persecuted for loving an Indian boy they tracked down and killed. Something changed then, something good came over the world. But here we are again, the same old fairy tale, the one in which I learn and you don't, our children still cast to the lions. And so, though you could be my Prince—I remember how we talked and danced—the answer is as before. I can't remove your mask for you.

NAVARRO BLUFF

My children and I live in a cabin on a two hundred foot Pacific Ocean bluff. The road on which we live is called Navarro Bluff Road, a remnant of old Highway 1, now a few hundred yards west of the new highway. Recently I found a sign under the house—*"Navarro Cliffs, The Ormsbees."* My landlord, Rollin Ormsbee, tells me it used to swing from the bullpine at the top of the steep drive until he gave up battling the wind that blew it down every month or so. The bluff, or cliff, forms the south lip of the mouth of the Navarro River and is one of those places you can't help but ponder the geological process. Friends who visit are often moved to describe to me the way mountains are worn down by water, churned under by ocean and pushed back up again as mountains. Still, the Navarro flows only about thirty miles from runoff creeks and springs around Anderson Valley. Further east in the coast range, the Ukiah Valley drains to sea, seventy miles south of the Navarro, the far more impressive Russian River. The Navarro, like the Russian, is tidal and floods nearly every rainy season, making Highway 128 impassable for a few days. Old-timers, my landlord among them, still recall with scorn the Highway Department's construction of 128 along the river in 1924. The original road ran along the top of Navarro Ridge, merging with the present highway near Floodgate Store, ten miles inland. Floodgate is at the confluence of streams that births the mature Navarro.

Rollin Ormsbee was born eighty-eight years ago, some fifteen miles east and north of the Floodgate Store in a place his father settled, Peachland. Today the only indication that Peachland ever existed is a highway sign at the west end of Anderson Valley,

Peachland Road. This narrow dirt road climbs to the former settlement and homestead where Rollin was born and raised. Rollin says of his father and the fate of Peachland: "He'd cut and mill a tree a month. Lasted about twenty-five years. Then he tan-oaked. Then he couldn't make a living anymore off the land. Happened to everybody. So he sold out, moved on." Rollin's family regarded Ukiah, the seat of Mendocino County, their town for shopping, schools, church, etc. rather than the much closer community of Boonville. Ukiah was eighteen miles from Peachland, Boonville six—this in the days of horse and wagon. "We were outlanders. They spoke their own language." This language was Boontling, one of the true oddities of local history, developed by the settlers of Boonville, situated on the tourist road to the coast, 128, to do just as Rollin's family experienced: to keep outsiders out.

Rollin built the cabin twenty-five years ago as a summer/weekend/retirement place. He and his wife have lived all their married life in Ukiah where he worked as an accountant for Mendocino County. Over the door of the garage is the date *November 7, 1953.* I am struck by this date because it is just eleven days before my grandmother died, a woman of their generation and the only relative outside my immediate family I knew as a child.

We lived on the ocean previously, three years on Topanga Beach in Southern California, so I was prepared for the opinions and reactions of others when we moved here. Even in Southern California most people cannot fathom living so close to so much water. They wonder how you stand the cold, the wind, the fog, the banging, crashing, bursting, exploding, blasting, cracking, popping, knocking, slapping, booming, rumbling, thundering, hissing, swishing, poofing of the tidal sea, and the moaning foghorns. Here, of course, the weather is far more extreme than in the south. The residents are sharply divided into the sunbelt personalities, those who have to live at least two miles inland, up the ridges and out of the fog, and those fewer of us who love the sea in all its conditions. Except for two years in Vermont, I have always lived on or near the Pacific Ocean. I was conceived on Redondo Beach and born in Seaside Hospital in Long Beach, so the sea I think is a condition of my being. In Vermont there were deep snowy days when I could smell the iodine of the ocean, a fact that would be verified by the weather report: an unusual easterly off the Atlantic.

Some of the Pacific's more dangerous aspects here have been chronicled. For instance, it is approximately every one hundred-and-fiftieth wave that is the killer wave, that sweeps innocent souls off the rocks and boats against them. We've lived in the area for less than four years and two of these in the woods, but even so I have witnessed two such tragedies. I've never been in the right place, however, to see one of the more legendary sights: the bluffs covered in white foam like snow from the high-flying, hard-crashing waves of a winter storm.

There is the story of a friend whose mother lives with her in a large glass structure over the Little River Blowhole. The face of the house is in alignment with the sheer rock face of the bluff. My friend's mother has mentally roped-off the front of the house, the living room, dining room, kitchen, and the omnipresent sea. She conducts her life in the back of the house and will not, for any circumstance, venture into the front. Another acquaintance, aghast at my new location, told of living in the Dolphin House on a bluff in Caspar, a house with two wooden walls sculpted as dolphins. A wreck anyway from the noise of the sea, he moved out the day a gigantic wave broke through the bay window. However, other friends, lovers of the sea, jumped at the chance then to live in this house.

When we first moved in Rollin kept warning us of what was to come. A few years ago he sealed off the south entrance to the cabin because the wind kept blowing it open. Last year, the house nearest us, on the south, lost its roof and "several tons of material" landed a hundred yards or so north of us. He kept emphasizing the natural disaster clause in my lease, assuring me that I would not be responsible for whatever happened to the place. In fact, this winter the storms were so fierce the roofs of several friends collapsed on them,

Noyo fishing harbor was declared a "disaster area" by the government—one whole dock with boats attached was swept to sea—and the windows of the new house highest on Navarro Bluff were blown out. My children sleep in the back rooms but I built my bed into the front corner windows and though I didn't get much sleep those nights, for fear of the windows breaking over me and the sea rushing three sides of me, for fear of Orion burning right through me with his eerie, cosmic light, I was delighted in the morning for having ridden out the storm.

Many nights the sea has awakened me, sometimes simply by its presence, an immense, inexorable beast, breathing under me, over me, biding his sweet time in the voyeuristic pleasure of watching Earth, until, growing bored or angry, or whatever, he moves to take me. Sometimes I'm awakened by his sudden silence, feel the dark tunnel of the sucking tide of death. I think of Rollin withdrawing from Earth, I think of certain friends sinking into the dark hills, the redwood and pygmy forests, my own life and death and the earth turning over to a new generation, glimpse our dissolution like the rich soil after the violence of heavy logging: how, with the first rains, the water at the mouth of the Navarro is the color of flesh. Push and then pull, the sea so like the heart I find myself saying the word *heart-sea* over and over. Once in a slam of a killer wave against the bluff I heard my son say from sleep, "Where are we going?" And still another night: "Now I'm getting scared." I look out my window on such nights, north up the bluff to the only other occupied cabin here, a woman who from the distance looks like me and whose light is often burning also at three and four in the morning. For all our isolation here, for the amazing thing we share, we have never met. Our friendship is the space of this bluff, the tidal changes of the sea, a bond neither of us seems moved to break with intimacy: her light between me and chaos. Once at Toad Hall, the local dance place in the redwoods, a man introduced himself to me as her lover. He wanted me to know that he used to live here too, but she needed to be alone even though she still loves him. It is on these nights that I have known if I ever write a book about Mendocino it will be a love story. For it is here, in this place of true outlanders and real lovers, that I have come to understand the Revolution is our lovelives.

And so you see what it is that moves me about my landlord and his wife, a couple whose temperaments, even in retirement, sought out and embraced such a wild and unpredictable place. Before land prices became sky-high it was a tradition with Mendocino County workers to build retirement cabins on the coast—just as it was the tradition for the inland Pomos to come here for relief from the summer heat. The Ormsbees' friends built their places in the pygmy and redwoods. "We stayed in a few," Rollin says, "just to make our friends happy. They all thought we were crazy to build on the ocean. They didn't have any imagination." There are ten cabins on Navarro Bluff which, with the exception of ours and the blond woman's, are only occasionally occupied, a settlement known locally as Little Geyserville, sometimes Geyserville-By-The-Sea. According to Rollin the land was originally a real estate deal in Geyserville, a small vineyard community eighty miles inland. All the cabins have fifty-foot lots that run from the road to the edge of the bluff, and all but our cabin hug the road. Rollin built his cabin right down in front of everyone, right on the western edge, "as close to the sea as possible," with its full view, among other spectacles, of the San Andreas Faultline where it disappears into the sea fifteen miles to the south. "The walls of the house, the white wood, is hemlock from the Cascasdes. It was new in '53. The lumbermen thought it a good thing. Well, it's fine when it's dry, but once it gets wet, no good. Had to replace the front of the cabin with redwood." A few steps down the bluff is a platform and bench that Rollin built. Every time Rollin visits he mentions how he and his wife used to sit on the bench drinking coffee. "This is where we visited each other," he says.

Once in late fall he and I sat there together, drinking coffee, watching the gray whales migrating to Baja. He said it was the sixtieth anniversary of his unit's march down Market Street before going to Europe to fight World War I. It was the first year he was missing the reunion because he could no longer drive. "Only it was called The Great War then," he said, a slight annoyance in his voice. "That was before the second one so it didn't have no number." This was the event in Rollin's life that caused him to lose his faith in God and all belief in an afterlife. "The Great Flu hit. I was in Pittsburgh. They stacked the bodies six high outside against the hospital walls. So cold it froze 'em. Can't ever forget those stacks. Always did suspect that flu was germ warfare." A whale spyhopped before us. It rose up out of the sea, up out of the humping and spouting of the others, until it was completely emersed, stood on its fluted tail, twisted to look up and then down the coast, and at us it seemed, then slowly screwed its gray barnacled self back down. Seagulls were flying beneath us. Rollin said, the afternoon sun suddenly out from a cloud, shining full on his corrugated face, "Those seagulls, always been mysterious to me. They're always flying north. All day they fly north. You go to sleep and the next day they are still flying north." I sit on the bench myself at least once a day, no matter how foul the weather, and have never failed to think of Rollin and his wife visiting each other here. Or of noting, that it seems to be true, since 1953 anyway, the seagulls fly only to the north.

Six years ago Rollin's wife had a stroke. That's when he began renting out the place. She was expected to die and he couldn't bear to come here without her. I understood this since I myself had turned down my first opportunity to rent it, even though I had long wanted the place. I was newly broken from a man I had been with for many years and still loved. Perhaps it is insensitive to compare this with Rollin's inability to live here again, but it was my first understanding of how painfully mocking beauty can be when you've lost someone you love. Perhaps this is why we as a species, with our innate sense of loss, are hellbent on destroying beauty. The poet Robin Morgan says, "Love is the process by which the beloved's face is kindly interposed between the lover and chaos." A close friend visited me not long after her husband had been killed in a car accident. I met her in San Francisco, we spent the day in the city, drove the three-hour road in the night. I was moved with how well she was handling her grief. But the next morning when she woke to the sun lighting the coastline north and south, and the vast expanse of silver sea with its luminous gunmetal horizon line, she collapsed in tears. "It's too beautiful," she kept crying. "It's *too* beautiful."

And Rollin says it every time he comes, "Oh, my wife, she loved this place. When I was still working for the county, I'd get off at five and we'd leave by six. She'd have the car packed with food and things. We'd get over here after dark and stay until after dark on Sunday. After I retired we came over for four or five days a week. We have a lovely modern home in Ukiah, but she preferred it here." During another visit he told me of the earthquake of 1906 when he was sixteen. He was awakened early in the morning in Peachland, saw out the window a thick old oak tree bending in two at the trunk, "like a rubber band," all the way to the ground. It wasn't spring yet but the first gray whales, the mothers with their newborn calves, were already returning to Alaska. Then he told me what it's like now with his wife.

The doctors said there was no hope for her surviving the stroke. But she's lived for six years, her condition unchanged from the first day. She is bedridden, can't talk and apparently understands little of what is going on around her. He visits her at the convalescent home every day between 10:30 and 11, only a half hour so as not to tire her, recalling how exhausted he once was after a car accident on Covelo Road, his friends tormenting him with their overly long visits to the hospital. For a long time he couldn't tell if she recognized him, or was aware of his presence. He tried many ways to communicate with her, but she remained unresponsive to everything he or the doctors and nurses tried.

Then he remembered that she loved apples. "Apples and Navarro Bluff were her greatest loves," Rollin said. "Of course, when we were young you could only get apples in season and since she took care of the shopping I hadn't realized, what with modern technology, I could get apples any time of the year." So the next morning before his 10:30 visit, he walked to the supermarket and bought an apple. "They don't call them supermarkets for nothing." Then he walked to the home, into her room, took out his pocket knife, quartered the apple the way she always did, and handed the piece to her. There was a long moment in which Rollin more or less gave up. She didn't know he was there. He sat down, with the apple quarter extended to her, sank into his own trance. "Sometimes she hypnotizes me." But then, without looking at him, or making any other sign, Mrs. Ormsbee began moving her hand toward the apple. Very slowly she took the slice from her husband, moved it to her mouth, and began eating it.

Thus it has been now for six years for the couple that sought out this rugged bluff, who sat daily over this two-hundred-foot western edge of the North American continent, over the San Andreas Faultline, over this truly wild end of the world, to visit each other. If I were an adequate storyteller I could tell this story with something akin to a happy ending. As another octogenarian friend told me when I finally asked why he continues to live—a highly educated man who mourns that he can no longer read or walk out in sunlight, or make love to women, his greatest sorrow, and who has difficulty with his memory—"Because it's something else. Living is none of these things. It's something else."

Something as illusive and mysterious as the seagulls at Navarro Bluff that are always flying north. "Every day," Rollin says, "between 10:30 and 11, I take an apple quarter to my wife and she eats it. It is how we visit with each other now."

LIFE IN THE GREAT NORTHWEST SOMEWHERE

Carlos

It's different now. In '69 and '70 when I came here,it was different, different energy. We just came here. Our karma brought us here. We were straight out of the city. Brooklyn working class. I said I was never going back, left with $200. It seemed a lot. Got here with ten and a fifty dollar bill folded up inside my belt buckle. Yeah, three of us, all the way across the country for the first time, cramped into my VW. And a dog, an Irish Setter named Berserk. Harold was 24, had never been out of the city, never been north of the Bronx in his life. Yeah. It still happens. People trapped in the city all their lives. We came to the coast, Huntington Beach first. *Fuck!* I'd dreamed of the Pacific all my life, I couldn't believe it, there were steel cranes out in the water, buildings right up to the edge. So we got out of there. Not till we got to Rincon Beach, north of Santa Barbara, did we come to a beach like I thought the Pacific would be. Then we came here, and suddenly we were all building houses. We were workers. Just started helping people build houses everywhere. No idea how to do it. Kenny was getting these huge thirty-foot redwood beams three feet around for a dollar and gypsies like us just kept coming through from all over the country, wanting to help build. They started in the summer. Harold, Harry and I arrived in the fall. Maybe I'd go to town once or twice in six weeks. Mendocino, yeah, to town. Just stayed on the land and worked. It was crazy, the energy unreal. None of us knew what was happening. We were just doing it. Winter was coming and everyone was looking for a welfare mother to shack up with. And then I found myself in a van with six others going to Mexico. We were figures out of a Tarot pack.

Albion River Flats
September 2, 1974

◇ ◇ ◇

Two Old Women Behind Me

There's a Mendosa. 12th grade, a Senior now. Mendosas, one of us. And lookie there! That old fellow's the one who built our barn. Imagine. He's still here too. Course the barn isn't. The state took it for the park. My father, he came here from Denmark, he always was telling me who lived where in the beginning, which houses, and the maiden names. He always said try and remember the maiden names. He always was saying the maiden names should be legalized so we won't forget. He always said it was important not to forget. He had all those photos in the attic. Wish I had them now. That house has been torn down too of course. All those old houses. I just don't like it, I don't like it at all. Like the house that's now The Windfall. The washroom is still there, luckily. I get a kick out of my old Annie talking about restoring this town. She says for $21,000. But that won't solve the problem of the hippies. Hippies. Hippies everywhere.

Mendocino Bank of America
October 9, 1974

◇ ◇ ◇

Little River Postmaster

There's no word in the regulations for postmistress

People have offered us a hundred thousand for it. Imagine. It's really falling down. I try to tell them. I guess because it's on the ocean side of 1.

But you know if we sold it, even for that kind of money, where would we go?

I was born in Big Bear, California. Know where that is? It was a good place to grow up. Lake Arrowhead. But my father moved here when he saw the smog coming.

I used to walk to work. Every day. Started here in 38. But not now! Same road, but the traffic. The logging trucks!

Little River Post Office
October 16, 1974

◇ ◇ ◇

Hitchhiker: Running Dog

I'm going down to LA. Have to go to the city here to find out what time the bus leaves. Can't get anyone on the line, they won't answer their phone. Got my ticket but can't find the time. I'm staying at the Albion Community Center with the brothers and sisters there. I stay in the metal shack out back.

I'm going down to LA to see about somethin. How about you, brother, want some of this here port?

I was up in Demming awhile, bought a gold mine. Haven't worked it yet. Gonna work it this spring. Use a chemical retract, retract the gold, $200 an ounce, you know. That's a lot of money. If you can't see the gold in the bottom of the pan you throw it out. At $200 an ounce you can't afford to do that. With chemicals you get it. It's for my children's education. Leave them something.

It ain't easy goldmining.

Half-breed myself. From Canada and Detroit. Quebec. Raised on a reservation there. Canuck. You have to be French and Indian to be Canuck. Quebec is separate from Canada, they don't need Canada. In 1964 the Queen came to Canada. She sent her forerunners up and said to block our people from speaking Canuck. It's not in the books. She told the people there with the cafes don't feed the people who order in Canuck. Well, we burned down a few of the agent buildings there as she was coming up and her advisors said she shouldn't. Why not? she said. I'm their queen.

You are not their queen. They are of the frontier. They can't recognize you as their queen. They have men on either side of the road up in those hills with rifles and bow and arrows, they'll get not only you but everyone that goes with you.

Finally she realized her intelligence and decided not to go.

The reservations in Canada are different from here. Here they fight with one another over government grants. It's greed, that's what it is. There, if one man has a dollar it's for everyone. Everyone works together. It's the way it should be.

You can let me off in the city here at Captain John's. Do you know Captain John? From Finland, yeah he's the old man who walks around town in a sea captain's cap. He helps the brothers and sisters when they get here and don't have anything to eat, lets them sleep here in his yard on Main Street. He's helped out a lot of the brothers and sisters. He helped me out when I first came here. I don't forget a friend. I'm going to say goodbye now.

Highway 1, North Side of Albion Bridge
to Mendocino, my son and I.
September 27, 1975

◇ ◇ ◇

Maximilian Rainbow, Highway 1 And The Car Radio

Listen! That's Billy Eckstein. Remember him? Billy Eckstein, you know, the Forties. Our mothers liked him.

Did I ever tell you about Rudy, the Mexican guy I was in jail with? The guy who wanted to marry me? In jail for heroin. He told me about Billy Eckstein. He was Billy Eckstein's pusher, and a woman singer's, maybe Billy Holiday. He had stories of riding around LA in cars with Billy, going to his apartment, things like that.

Once in 1949 the cops pulled him out of his car, beat him up, broke his jaw. If you sell any more dope to Billy Eckstein we'll kill you. They didn't do nothin to Billy Eckstein. They liked him. He was their Negro singer victim. Rudy was their evil pusher.

He's the same guy who was coming through Mexico with three mules carrying dope. A dope caravan. And they came up over a rise and there sit the Mexican police on horseback, rifles pointed at them.

The same guy who was on a bus going through Idaho during the war. Passed a U.S. Army base. He saw acres and acres of marijuana growing. Couldn't believe his eyes. Turned out to be the government's hemp crop.

The same guy who was trying to get the hospital dope program I was trying to avoid. You get out sooner, but you have seven years of heavy-duty parole. Naline urine tests, if you have any heroin in you you go into convulsions. But they kept telling him he was too old to be rehabilitated. Best they could give him was fifteen to life.

I was 25 then. His son was 25. He used to tell me the only thing you can do, kid, is teach your kids to hate cops. His son was in Leavenworth for armed robbery.

The dopers, you know, have the highest status in jail. Yeah. I was in for six pounds. There were guys in for one joint. So I had status. The burglars were the lowest. They hung out in the back, sneaky-like, sullen. The dopers are intelligent, got a little class, know about art, people respect them, give them their graham crackers, milk, things like that.

I was in during the Watts Riots. The guys kept coming in beat-up, their Achilles' heals sliced from climbing in broken window fronts. Looters. But when you'd ask them what they in for they'd say robbery in Inglewood. They were ashamed to be looters then. That was before Eldridge Cleaver told them to be proud. I was on the fourteenth floor of Old LA County and I could see the flames. It was hairy, I was afraid they'd get me, had to keep telling myself that I'd been ok to all the blacks.

But I was glad. Did my heart good, see those flames. I wanted the whole fuckin town to burn.

The police were scared too. They brought in ice cream. Two nights in a row. *Ice cream!* Some of us boycotted it, kissin our asses. Didn't want no riots on their hands, nervous, it was funny. Usually, it was Hey, trustee, your bed ain't made. Hey, trustee, take that pencil out your ear. They'd promise, then never bring you aspirin when you had a headache. Suddenly treatin us like grandchildren with the Watts Riots goin on.

One month of my year was at New County. Eleven months at Old County. Old County was best, funkier. You could have graham crackers and milk in your cell at night. New County, they didn't want no rats. Old County you could leave the window open. Downtown LA smog was better than no windows at New County. Piped air that was always too warm. And smelled. The cafeteria clock at New County was always disconnected. Probably so you wouldn't know how short your eating time was.

The radio sound system at Old County was donated by Robert Mitchum after he did time there in the 40s for dope. Rudy could remember the old sandstone police building on 1st Street.

I met an old man who had been in there in '26. First time back again, '65. An old alcoholic. I was in the cell with him when he got the news his wife had been killed in an apartment house fire. We spent days locked in with him grieving. Probably drinking and smoking, he said. She fell asleep. Telling us for days what a wonderful woman she had been, how beautiful and successful she was in high school. And just days before he had been cussing her cause she wouldn't bail him out, how he was gonna beat her up when he got out. The cop that brought him the news promised him a phone call to find out more about it, talk to the hotel manager, see to her body, but he went off duty and the guy on night shift said he didn't know nothin about it.

I saw him later during a peace march, sitting on a curb at MacArthur Park, looking confused.

And Rudy. He wanted to marry me. I wonder where he is now.

Look at that little town! Those clouds over it like the Grand Canyon. Must be prettiest town on earth.

You know? He might still be in there.

Albion to Mendocino
October 4, 1975

◇ ◇ ◇

Carrie Furth On Independence Day

Are you gonna have a jolly Fourth, honey? My friends are concerned mine will be too poppin. Goin out to the lake at Lucerne. Picnic and fire works. Once in a lifetime event, the Bicentennial Independence Day.

I guess up in Willits they're havin a bash. Nine days of celebratin. A raucous blowout. Never been there myself.

I'm from Mendocino. The south coast. It's called Manchester. North of Pt. Arena. Dairy farms. Well, the girls got married, you know. My boy is girl-shy, one of these days. He's 28. Well, you know, he better not be losin time.

Well, I came here cause of teeth problems, you know, doctors n all and they say I had a nervous breakdown.

But I love it where I am. This hotel.

Furth. Mrs. Archie Furth. Old family. Archie's well-known on the coast. My first name? Carrie. But it's Archie's name that's known.

The Ladies Room of the Black Bart Room
The Palace Hotel, Ukiah
June 30, 1976

◇ ◇ ◇

The Man Who Saved Mendocino

I'm through. I'm just through. I've had it. Backlash. There's this backlash. I get poison pen letters in the mail. The doctor told me I was through any minute if I didn't get out. I felt like I was born in a different body the minute I said *Ok, I'm through*. It was hard, figuring out what to do next. I applied for a fellowship, going to Rome now. Just a student now.

It's been something, these seventeen years. Incredible. It was a ghost town when we came here. The demise of active lumbering was in '43. By mid-fifties, Mendocino was a ghost town. You know what the bankers said to me? They said Mendocino is dead and we want it to stay dead. But we got the $500 for the down somehow before those two guys from Fort Bragg could make a trailer court out of what is now the Art Center. We were artists from the city, late '50s, a beautiful exodus, oh, we had such hope. The natural beauty here, of course, there's no place in the world as beautiful. They make movies here. You know the house of prostitution in *East of Eden*? That's the house that was on the property before the fire. Anyhow we jacked up six old carriage houses. Al and I built this apartment. No public money, some donations, all volunteer labor, everything by cash, any community could do this. I have the plans drawn up. Anyone who wants can use them. But I'm sick and tired. I showed every Wednesday night movie for fifteen years. I can't go in that room now, it makes me ill. I get poisoned pen letters! I can't believe it. They kill me. Let me tell you I put my heart and soul into this town. Two old women talking before the stove, warming their feet, one foot at a time, the roof not in yet, that was the beginning. Oh, it was good, the creative energy, the art. Now they say I ruined this place.

The Mendocino Art Center
October 2, 1976

◇ ◇ ◇

April, Her Last Name Means Power

At first when he left me I wasn't here. There was this wall of tears between me and the world. I couldn't see.

And then the world started growing up from the ground.

Leaving Jack London's ranch
Valley of the Half-Moon
April 20, 1977

◇ ◇ ◇

The Pygmy Forest

There's something in it. I wouldn't want to *live* in it. Myself, I can't stay in it more than a half hour. Some strange spirit is in it, something weird, lives in the soil maybe. I mean it *grows* in the shadow of redwoods. But these people who haul in soil from other places, grow their food in it, go to sleep in it at night, want to subdivide it, think they own it, aren't sensitive to it—or *think* they're not, anyway. Some sort of closure in their skin. Even lovers of redwoods won't fight for it. Some love it, I guess, but that's rare. I mean it's not just because it's so rare you'd want to save it, little pockets of it from Fort Bragg to Navarro, and no where else in the whole world, maybe some place in Russia, it's that something's out there, something lives in it. For me, something not even pleasant, but something I'm sure, important, maybe even necessary. Makes you wonder what's being done to people who live in it, don't even realize they're living in it, but think they own it. No skin's so tough, I'm sure, not to be touched by it. They want to kill it.

Richard, G. Road, Albion
May 6, 1977

◇ ◇ ◇

Well-Known American Poet

Drove-up from Fairfax. Shared the driving with Larry here. He drove as far as Cloverdale, 101. Then I took over. 128. What a road, the curves. Being drunk. But *pretty*. But as bad as that goddamn freeway. Worse. We had to stop at every bar along the way. When we got to Mendocino I stopped at the Shell Station, a trick I learned when I played pool. Yeah, I was a pool shark at 18, played up and down the Mississippi River. Yeah, on gambling boats. A trick to get my nerve back. Ten push-ups. I went into the men's bathroom. *Piss all over the floor!* Well. You got to do it in the piss of men. I got down there in the piss of men. I did ten pushups in the piss of men. Then I did five more. Then I knew I was still together. And then I was ready for Mendocino.

The Foghorn Tavern, Mendocino
May 14, 1977

◇ ◇ ◇

You Have The Face I Wanted My Mother To Have

We're acting out in our lovemaking incestuous roles. She imagines I'm her father, her son. I imagine she's my mother, my daughter.

I don't remember my real mother. But when I was twelve my father took me to Maine and told me—my mother waving goodbye from the brownstone steps in Brooklyn—that my real mother was dead.

He was going off to work one morning, she was collapsing on the kitchen floor. The autopsy showed she died early in the morning. When he returned that night, I was a baby clinging to her cold dead body.

Maybe this is why I cling to women now.

Zen Poet
Port Townsend, Washington
July 12, 1977

◇ ◇ ◇

April Hooked

I saw him in the SeaGull. Or rather, really, I saw his silver hooks, one clasping a wine glass. I couldn't help but stare. The beauty of his silver hook around the silvery stem of a glass of white wine, *oh!* I went right over, put my head down between his two hooks and said, *Oh. Wow.* He followed me home. I told him there was no way I was going to fuck him. He said he was a pirate and had every intention of fucking me. I laughed, he was a fool. I'd been celibate for six months. He quoted pirates, Long John Silver, Ahab, Bluebeard on making love to women. After that it seemed easy to ask him.

How did you lose your hands?

He said he'd been a real macho character, an adventurer. He was hanggliding. Something happened. He was falling. The ground was coming. He grabbed onto a high tension wire. It burned off both his hands. He was dead. He looked back to his body hanging on the wire. Then he saw his friend climbing the pole to rescue him. His body was hot. He screamed *Don't touch me!* Like that, he was back in his body. Alive.

I wondered then how he'd touched me.

Navarro Bluff
November 14, 1977

◇ ◇ ◇

Have You Ever Seen Steelhead Rising?

We live on Low Gap Road, off the Comptche-Ukiah Road. Fifteen miles west of Ukiah but it takes an hour to drive to Ukiah, an hour and a half to get here to the coast. We came over tonight to see the sun set, to escape the heat, 111°. 117° in Covelo someone said. We figured it'd be like this. Can you believe? This fog? And windy! It's cold.

We're fixing up an old ranch. Eighty acres. I'm a Taurus, May 19, 1941. You can tell, how large I am. These levis. Bill here, he's my husband, he's 46, an ex-writer. He says I'm earthy. He likes my face, brown and weathered. My big ass. Once he met Jack Kerouac. He always says the thing about Kerouac is that he *believed*, absolutely, in everything he said. Everything. A complete innocent in some tragic way. My husband quit writing in 1968 after finishing a novel. It was on the order of *Zen And The Art Of Motorcycle Maintenance*. It was before its time. He says only a fool would keep writing if he didn't sell. But he still pines for the writer's life.

I'm a Taurus. I don't do nothing. Nothing. Absolutely nothing. Never had children.

You really want to know what my day is like?

You *really* want to know?

Well. First thing. I get fucked. *Ha-ha-ha!* Then I make breakfast, do the dishes, dust a little, make lunch. Then comes siesta. And I get fucked again. Then I work some on the house, panel the rooms, a little carpentry. Then I fix dinner, we eat, and then we go to bed. And I get fucked again. *Ha-ha.*

Oh, sometimes I go down to catch steelhead. Our land is on the South Fork of the North Branch of the Navarro River. At its source. But the steelhead, by the time they get to us, through Masonite, Louisiana Pacific, are so fucked up, their poor bodies so battered, you don't have the heart to fish for them. Have you ever seen salmon rising for you? That's what the steelhead do. They rise half out of the water, and look at you. Of course, if steelhead are like salmon, it's all a part of the breeding process. All they're doing, like me, is fucking. Their whole life. Right to the end.

Caspar Inn, Caspar
August 9, 1978

◇ ◇ ◇

Mechanics

I'm buried beneath the hood of the Limo, my elbows sticking out, *up* to them in grease, trying to figure out what's wrong with the spark plug and why the fuck Jonah would have put in one that didn't match, when a woman approaches me. First I see the high heels, matching purse. She's wearing make-up and new clothes and she asks, *Do you need any help?*

Robin, Mendocino Village
February 18, 1979

◇ ◇ ◇

Sailor

It's called ghosting. No one knows this, only you do: *there's no sound at four knots.* You're *within* the wind. The Sioux name for horse is *Within The Wind.* Your energy is wind, the same speed as wind.

There's a push from behind that lifts you. Whether you're on water, snow, ice or land. Because the Earth is just a vast lake, and you rise. And you rise.

Miguel, The Oasis, Elk,
March 22, 1979

◇ ◇ ◇

Bringing Him Beer

You don't remember me, do you? I saw you dance two years ago at the Anchor Inn. I've never forgotten. You danced by yourself. I saw butterflies coming out of your fingertips. I had never seen anything like it. I had never seen anything so beautiful. You inspired me to dance. People think you're crazy when you dance by yourself, particularly for a man. But I would just see you again dancing at the Anchor Inn two years ago and it would give me courage and inspiration. I've been dancing ever since. I've been in the South. They think you're crazy there to dance by yourself, but I'd just visualize you.

I've been dancing for two years now, up and down the Eastern Seaboard. I've been winning the contests.

When I won first place at the *Club 2001*—the *Club 2001*? You've never heard of it? It's the biggest disco in the world, at Pensacola—when I won first place I married the cocktail waitress. The first time we talked I told her about you, how you dance. I told her about Fort Bragg, this place where you can dance by yourself and no one thinks you're crazy. So I brought her back here. She was young, 19. She was killed on Highway 20 three months ago.

Logging truck hit her, coming around one of those curves. She was from Florida. Flat land.

I thought it was bad before, all that shit with my son Tahoe. Remember my son? How I kidnapped him from his mother, hid him up here. I thought it important that he live here. I thought it important to bring my wife here.

But Fort Bragg doesn't seem like it did two years ago. It's changed. Don't you think it's changed?

January 14, 1980
Tip Top Lounge, Fort Bragg

◇ ◇ ◇

Willow

You remind me of my cousin, Trudy. Oh, you make me miss my cousin, Trudy. I can never remember your name, but you remind me of my cousin. She's not so thin. You're thinner in the cheek area.

She's had a hard life, but not because she's bad. She's good.

I don't understand. Her karma hasn't come around yet. Her mother, my aunt killed herself two weeks before her wedding. She called my other aunt, she called my mother, Listen! I've just got to talk to someone. No one had time. So she went down stairs and just hung herself.

There's an old superstition that you shouldn't get married til six months after a death in the family, but everyone said go ahead. Ten months after the wedding her husband was shot, right here, the left part of the heart by someone he didn't know. He was out in the woods driving a model T and they came up and shot him. They never were caught.

Then she married again. She doesn't lay around. It took her two years to find another, then she married, but then . . . oh, god, you remind me so of her, you make me miss her so much.

I'm from Michigan. I can take my mom about two days. I love my mom. But, you know. I was a vegetarian and she served a dinner of all meat: cows, pigs, chickens, fish. I said, Mom, I'm not going to eat that shit. She said, oh, yes, you are. I said, oh, no I'm not. She said, oh, yes you are. So I split. Just last year I went back for the first time. I missed her. I'm a gun freak now. Live in the woods in B.C., shoot all my food. So I told her I shot my own food. She *loves* meat. I thought she'd dig it. But she made me get out.

She can't forgive me cause of my baby. I was a junkie. I didn't believe in killing my own flesh, so I didn't have an abortion. My old man, he used me as a guinea pig to test all the stuff, cocaine, heroin and all, he was a dealer. But he stayed with me through the whole pregnancy. It wasn't his kid. I was 17. He was beautiful. He wanted a pretty white girl on his arm. I named her Fredericka Marie Rice. Fredericka was the name of the county I lived in. My mother's name is Mary, but I always thought it was really Marie. I was a junkie. I found a family for her.

Now I'm a gun freak. I kill, skin all my meat. I live like a squaw. Wear out my moccasins fast. See these holes: that's two hours on the sidewalk in San Francisco. I'm leaving this place in the morning. That's why I'm drinking. I'm going back to my old man. Sequim, Washington. I'm sick of this place. It's like left-over LA. I'm going back to the woods. I've been gone from him a year. Even his mom says I shouldn't go back. She says he hasn't changed. He beats me. He beats me bad. But I can't tell if it's better with him or without him. I know one thing, he's the owner of my heart.

Caspar Inn, Caspar
April 18, 1980

◇ ◇ ◇

Growing Your Beard Back

Well, the first night I shaved I came in here and there was this very flashy beautiful woman, a blonde, who took me home.

The next morning I woke up next to her and realized I didn't want to be a part of the Upper Mendocino Shuffle.

The SeaGull Cellar, Mendocino
April 21, 1980

◇ ◇ ◇

The Only Place We Got Left

I been coming to this lake forty years. Native of San Francisco, there's a few of us left. Mendocino? I used to go hunting, fishing up there, forty years ago. The town? I can't remember a *town* called Mendocino. I know Elk, Alder Creek, Fort Bragg, Point Arener, the Russian River north. We'd go up. We just did it. The normal thing, when the abalone and steelhead ran. We'd hit the Russian River first, then work our way north, fish the Garcia, then Alder Creek, Land's End, up to Pt. Arener, past the Reservation. You ever heard of Olsen? No. Probably not. Before your time. He owned all that land there. He didn't have no fences, just the land ending. His sheep ran wild, the other livestock. Wild horses, wild pigs, wild cows.

And fog! I'd get out with two flashlights, one in each hand and lead the car up that road. It runs right off the cliff there into the ocean. Nobody'd ever find you. The buddy I went with, he'd been raised on the Reservation. Shit, it ain't nothin now. The Reservation. Course, then, it was mostly Klamath River tribes. We'd go up to their Round House where they'd have ceremonies and things. At Alder Creek there. Let me tell you. I know where the Indians planted their corn. Their maize.

My buddy. He got a good job in San Fran. As soon as he saved the money he bought his parents a nice little house in Fort Bragg, moved them there. And there they lived to the end of their happy days. The Reservation's nothing now. Now it's called a *Rancheria*. Nothin now. Nothin. They get $30 a month to stay there. A government penance. Oh, it's terrible. We used to load up the back of the car full of toys and clothes 'n' things, drive it up to the Reservation, throw the stuff out, and they'd scramble for it.

The North Coast is the only place we got left. Mendocino and Tahoe. Really. It's changed some, but not that much. You're really lucky, you know, to live there. You know, population explosion.

They all want to come to California. Well, that's okay, but it's sad. They put that road through the redwood trees. That hurt a lot. 101. We used to go up the old road, all the way to Eureka. Fortuna. In there. Klamath Falls. The Redwood Highway. It's still nice, but . . . .

Alder Creek. Do you know Alder Creek? We hunted quail up Alder Creek. They say it's the fault line. Everything south of it goes. Shit, it don't scare me none. I like it. The danger. I've lived on the fault line all my life. San Mateo. I'm a *western* Jew.

Henry Miller died today, didcha hear. 88. *88!* To be so lucky! You know what his last word was? *Mystery*. That's what I believe in. *Mystery*. It's my religion. I could tell you stories. I haven't even begun. The road up past Fort Bragg, to that town, the most northern town. Windport? I can't remember the name. Then it goes inland. Damn. It's our last place. Really. There and here. This lake. You won't believe this, but I used to *hunt* in Marin County. Now it's all churches and schools. *Churches and schools!* Right where I used to hunt. A church and a school.

Casa D'Cliffs
Incline Village
Lake Tahoe
June 8, 1980

Life in the Great Northwest is the name of a comic strip by Gilbert Mervinus.

UTAH RUN

He left in an old pickup with two other musicians two days before us. They went north out of Mendocino, 101 to 36 south of Eureka, then 3 through the Trinity Mountains. At Yreka they cut over to 97 and then crossed into Oregon. At Klamath Falls they cut east again to 395 and the long stretch of Oregon desert. They crossed the Idaho border at Ontario just south of Weiser where the fiddler's festival was happening. He called from Ontario. I was on my way out the door when the phone rang. The kids were waiting in the car. I watched the sun's high morning glare ripple across the sea as I listened to the plains behind him, now in him: the whine of highway in June, his speedy on-the-road voice, Oregon, Idaho, their dusty western echo through the lines. I could almost feel his two day beard scratching my face. He loved me. He missed me. We would meet in Idaho. Or in Salt Lake City. He would call me when we got there.

And so we set out in Roses, our American Motor stationwagon, David, Darien, our Alsatian shepherd, Moonlight, and as far as Sacramento, David's girlfriend. We drove up off Navarro Bluff, our last home in the fifteen we had known together. We took 128 through Anderson Valley. With the girlfriend directing we cut across at Petaluma, circled the lush oak backbay country I had not driven before. They sat quiet and serious in the backseat, the end of their high-school romance. We left her at her grandmother's, circled suburban streets, manicured lawns, the meaty trees, flat Sacramento of the great San Joaquin Valley, then rose up Donner Summit of the High Sierras. Before Reno as we reeled down into the numinous twilight of the desert one of the tires started thudding. A new retread, peeling. I knew one person in Reno. We found her, spent the night, borrowed some money for the tire. While the car was in the garage the three of us walked around Reno. It was Saturday morning. Darien, delighted at the sight of all the people in front of the slot machines, dropped in a dime before she could be stopped for being underage—she was fourteen—and in a single pull won five dollars.

The road from Reno goes almost due north to Winnemucca. Then east to Elko, KFI blasting from LA, David screeching out the window to the seagulls, *Life in the fast lane*. When night came, they slept, the two long beautiful bodies of my children asleep perhaps for the last time in the back of the car while I drive all night through strange country. This sleep on the road, the all-night motion of the car eating miles, the awakening in a new state, an unknown place: already they spoke of this experience as one of the wonders of their childhood. One of our homes had been a '60 Ford Falcon Stationwagon for six months. Home: the car and the road. At Wendover while they slept I stopped and looked down on the Great Salt Lake Desert. The border town neon flashing to Utah for alcohol lit the whole sky behind me. Moonlight romped in the arc of neon aureoles. I turned around to the northwest and wondered where Robin was, wondered how I'd ever be able to let David go to this desert. I looked in on him sleeping in the window next to his sister, their blond curls spread everywhere on the pillows. *My beautiful son, my football player.* I changed my thoughts quickly to Robin again, sang to him out there, over there, wherever, from Wendover, one of our songs, *Moonlight and Roses remind me of you.*

From those border cliffs you drop altitude drastically and the world changes. "White as snow and hard as cement," the map described it. Around two I stopped to sleep, not wanting to pull into Salt Lake while still dark. I parked beside the state historical marker for the Bonneville Salt Flats, *Site of Automobile Speed and Endurance Records* and an account of measuring the earth's curvature: how from this flat place you watch the racing cars disappear over it. The cracked crystalline salt bed shimmered in the starlight and the rising half moon. I let Moonlight out while I cleared the space in the frontseat. He ran across the monochromatic distance for what looked like drinking water. He was the same as the land, white as salt. In a minute he was back at my feet, whimpering. He stayed in the car the rest of the night. The place frightened him. I lay under the steering wheel with him wondering about Robin, listening to the sounds of my children sleeping. The semis bore down, then passed in a violent wind. I kept having to fight little moments of hysteria when it seemed I'd be overwhelmed with the impending loss. I thought again about Robin. I loved him. I missed him.

We were quiet as we went that morning into Salt Lake City. This was to be David's home now. We circled block after block. The University "U" painted on the face of the Wasatch, the western slope of the Rockies, flashes to the whole city. They wanted to eat hamburgers and tacos at the orange drive-in a block from the Mormon Temple. I let them off, found a parking place, changed in the front seat to my "straight" clothes and walked back through the Saints. The glassed fastfoods house was packed, it must have been close to noon or else everyone else was having hamburgers for breakfast. As I came around the corner I saw my reflection in the glass. The Temple's reflection, its gothic spires, filled the window in which the kids were sitting beyond me at an orange plastic table. When our eyes met we broke into hysterical laughter, me losing it right on the street. How funny we looked in Salt Lake City! My Levi skirt was not straight at all amidst all the pastel polyester. And they had far too much hair, gold aureoles around their neon bodies. They looked sinfuly healthy among the pale, timid souls of Burger King in Temple Square.

But Utah's football coaches were Southern California men, warm, humorous, and wise to the multitudinous ways of people. They delighted in telling the outragous stories of their recruiting trips to the Mendocino coast. *Hippy capital of the world,* they called it. We were nearly legendary by the time we got there, partly because I convinced David not to sign until June 1, long past the deadline. Every astrologer that year knew it would be suicidal for a Libra to sign a legal document before June 1. The head coach himself finally appeared on Navarro Bluff in a silver Cadillac carrying a pack of tarot cards in his suit pocket. He told me his grandmother had been the most famous gypsy tarot card reader in the country and hinted at other occult means for winning games. True or not, recruiting or not, it worked. David had been recruited by a dozen schools. This man's ingenuity, his sense of theater was rare among the men we had dealt with all winter, rare and of a quality we could relate to. And so he signed with Utah. Tight End. *After* June 1.

Darien and I stayed a few days with the line coach. His was one of the numbers I had given Robin. He gave us the grand tour of Utah's facilities. The thousand dollar seat section *was* impressive though the coach at that point seemed exasperated with me. "I just don't think you're comprehending how famous your son is going to be!" he said, throwing his enormous arms out over the empty stadium and all of Salt Lake City and desert beyond. Moonlight, chasing seagulls across the field below, stopped, turned to us, and barked in response.

I was getting some idea. On Sunday we drove north to Brigham City to attend a church dedication service for the son of one of my oldest friends. He was to depart the following week for Japan on his two year mission for the Church of Latter Day Saints. He and my son have known each other since they were babies. During the service for which I wore Una's Sunday clothes, high heels and nylons, make-up and a silky, slinky mauve dress, David was introduced over the elaborate P.A. system the Mormons use in their ceremonies. He received an enthusiastic ovation. It was as funny to me as dressing up sexy to go to church. The first church service of my son's life and he's lauded for being a football player.

Afterwards, David and I went fishing. Darien returned to Orem, south of Salt Lake, with the family. In Ogden he bought trout fishing gear with one of his graduation checks. We drove up North Ogden Canyon. I found a boulder next to him, barefoot, in my friend's mauve dress, and settled into a meditative quiet so the fish would bite. *Let him go,* I kept telling myself. I had feared this day for so long. The river was high and fast—most of the season's snow was still in the mountains—it rushed and spilled over the boulders around us. I remembered sitting with my father in Sierra canyons while he fished. I thought of the beach, lakes and rivers of David's childhood, and of Max, who had taught him to fish, the man David always said I had never gotten over. That David loved to fish, that he had always fished still surprised me. The silence, patience, solitude of the sport is contrary to his usual hyper, gregarious personality.

The two-lane highway through the canyon was thick with glarey, week-end traffic, mostly, it seemed, carloads of young men drinking beer. The sun seemed to drill us into the rock, the moment. Looking at him I could almost remember his father. He worked the new lure onto the hook, the light dancing off the metal, his beautiful, graceful hands. "Could be the best hands in the WAC," the coaches had said. I saw him, as I had once during the week, going out for a pass, the Wasatch Mountains behind him. How would I ever fill the loss of him in my days? I had been a child, younger than he was now, when I birthed him. Everything—my religion, my education, my politics, my way of living, my love life—stemmed from the astonishing moment he was first laid on my belly. Having suffered so much grief as a teenager from my parents I vowed then never to get on the other side of my child. That seemed to me, and still does, the essence of parenting, of love; it's as much a mystery to me now as then, how it happens so universally. It is not a mystery that it is not from love. Una had said this morning in front of the church. "You raise a boy to be the man you always wanted and then you have to let him go. It will be your greatest act of love." Actually, David had always seemed like me, the boy in me given the opportunity to live.

He had a bite. He reeled it in. I watched the old confusion play across his face, as the fish struggled in his hands. Once as a young boy in front of our Topanga Beach cabin he had caught a fish that birthed a half dozen babies as she was being reeled in, birthed them midair as if to free them to the sea. He had cried then. Now he said, adamantly, "Coach says I got to get my *Mean* together. He says it's going to be my biggest problem." He glanced at me as he had often in the past year, in actual appreciation, a conspiratorial grin to me, almost parenting. "He says it's because I was raised by a hippy mom." We laughed. A chunk of rock and soil fell into the river as he dropped the fish into the bucket. He laughed but I knew he wasn't confident about the meanness. To make the transition from his life on the Mendocino coast to being a football player in Utah was not going to be easy. To my mind it was a little like going to war, it seemed dangerous and therefore important for me to let him go for whatever truth there was in the coach's words. That night I dropped him off at the coach's house in the foothills behind Salt Lake. I saw again the erosion of the swift river. *Let him go.* I let him go.

We stayed a few more days in Orem with Una and her family, waiting for the phone call from Robin. It never came. At all the numerous shopping malls were posters for the Fiddler's Festival in Idaho. There were news stories on the radio and television. I called Navarro Bluff and Mendocino a number of times. No one had heard from him.

To make matters worse the chemistry between my friend and I had turned bad. Una and I were teenage mothers together. Though our beliefs are fundamentally opposed, our psyches have always transcended the obstacles of our clashing lifestyles. She calls me spouse of her soul. Recently she had sent me another Book of Mormon. *"To the one who has survived my husbands."* We wear different styles of clothes, we live in different kinds of houses, we have different ideas about these masks, but always we have managed to recognize each other. She is a mystic who spent most of her teenage years in the Utah State Mental Hospital for this "aberration." To me her Mormonism is the frame she's found to contain her awesome encounter with the universe. She said to me during this visit, "See that white spot three quarters up Mt. Timpanogos? The day after Johnny died I prayed for a sign. Then I saw him in the backyard. I went to my bedroom window and he was talking to me with Timpanogos filling the window behind him. On his left shoulder, beneath his chin, the white spot formed. It's been there ever since." Johnny Lookfar was Una's second husband. He was killed in a car accident on the road behind Timpanogos.

This time she quit speaking to me. This time the obstacles seemed greater than ever. Now our children were teenagers, my fourteen-year-old daughter gloriously mature without any of the strict discipline by which her girls, sixteen, fourteen, and ten were being raised, and to mind, crazed. Darien's presence was causing even greater dissension among them. *Why can't we date boys? Darien does!* Una screamed at them, grounding them for days for talking back to her. Now in the same week we were both losing our sons, our first-borns. We had gone through such crises before when we couldn't connect, but this time I needed her. I was lonely, bluesy, scared—where was Robin? Had he been in a car accident too? What was I going to do without my son? Was I being irresponsible, letting him be a football player in Utah? Would he be hurt? But Una wouldn't speak to me. *Better than being a missionary* I mumbled to myself as I watched her pack her son's things. His Temple garments, his sacred underwear.

I couldn't wait any longer for the call. I had to get out of there. Should we drive to Weiser? That had been one of our plans, but now it had been over a week. Somehow I knew he wasn't there. Somehow I knew he'd gone to Canada after another woman. That woman he went home with the night in March I wouldn't go to his gig.

It was night. I had to keep fighting the tears. I couldn't believe he'd do this to me. I wanted a drink, a smoke, something, a gentle word from my friend—hard commodities to come-by in Utah. I wandered out back. They were sitting in lawn chairs in the dark. Una got up and went back in the house, leaving me with Blacky, her new husband, a man I hardly knew. Blacky had been in the Utah Highway Patrol all his working life until recently when he received his BA degree and became a probation officer for the state. Something had happened a few months before and he had been fired. This was part of the current household strain, thirteen children between them and he was unemployed.

The peaks crowded in. You mow your lawn right up against the twelve thousand foot flanks, right around the celestial lights of Provo Temple. The white line of the ancient salt lake, Bonneville, is visible along the entire Wasatch front. Now the remaining Utah Lake stretched out, a silver-black mirror in front of us, the sky studded in it, a zillion stars. Suburbia in the wilderness. Brigham Young was right. This *is* some place. Blacky, apologetic for his wife, tried to talk to me. He asked me about David. Did I think he'd be okay? I could hear something coming in his voice. It would make a great book, he said several times.

He began to tell me a story. It was a long story that took me again to the road, to myself in Utah in a way I would not understand for a long time. I watched it unfold in the night as if I had gone to the movies for diversion in the middle of a personal crisis, or to sleep, as a dream or child from my sleeping body, the story spinning from the prone self without conscious narration, the self as viewer, listener, audience, utter creator and participant utterly taken from the life's main line. In dream after dream this is my story of the loss of my son and lover to Utah, the loss of myself to the road—the loss of myself to my story.

"There was this boy I knew, David Michaels. He was nineteen. After what happened I xeroxed all the records. They tell the whole story, a police record a mile long. It's all there in my desk if you want to see it. I've gone over and over it, I practically know it by heart. The kid just couldn't stay out of trouble. One of those, you know? In and out of trouble from twelve on, reform schools, state hospitals. But a real likable kid, good-looking, tall, dark, meticulously dressed. The dapper type, you know the type I mean? He wore *beautiful* clothes. But he was a thief. He bragged to me once that he'd shoplifted everything hanging in his closet. He said he started when he was nine, he got caught stealing bubblegum in a supermarket. His mother cried, he always mentioned this, his mother was crying right there in the market and he was hooked. They were from Massachusetts, he was born there. The father was an officer in the Navy, he moved the family to Brigham City when David was twelve to head the ROTC program at the college. That was part of it, I don't think he ever felt at home here. He had a lot of resentment about the Church. Guess you could, living here and not a Saint. Real soon after they got here he shoplifted something and his father turned him in. That's when he admitted many shiplifting incidents. After that episode it was cars and motorcycles. He was really into motorcycles. His fourteenth year he spent in the Utah State Mental Hospital here in Provo, same place Una was in. If he'd come from a poverty level family where a private psychiatrist couldn't have been used he'd have gone straight into the corrections system then. That would have straightened him out.

Though it's true, his father *was* traditional in his ideas of discipline. A military man. So I really don't understand what went wrong. Guess I never will. He always seemed close to his mother. For a while he was hooked on spray paint. She'd call me, 'Blacky, he's gone again.' He'd break into paint stores, right through the plate glass window, alarms wailing like cats and dogs, to get the paint. That's when he always had a line of paint across his face, a real beautiful boy. He'd hold a rag over the nozzle and spray right into his mouth and nose. Once, he was fifteen then, we found him naked, passed out in an abandoned barn. His clothes lay in a neatly folded pile beside him. We thought he was into some weird sex trip. Something funny. We took photographs. But later he explained. 'Oh, that's simple. My mom gets upset with me because the paint ruins my clothes, so I took them off.' You'll have to excuse me, I get choked up. He was a great kid. Once I took him with me on patrol, you know, thinking to change his perspective. We were sitting in this concealed spot out on 89. He said that car that just passed, that was a marijuana plant in the back window. We checked it out, sure enough, it was. He'd have made a good law enforcement officer. He had a good eye."

"But he couldn't stay out of trouble. He'd do great in the programs they had for him. A natural leader. Everyone loved him. He'd get what he could out of them, but then he'd be bored. For a while he was with a real nice Mormon family but they couldn't handle him. He'd come home stoned out of his gourd. They loved him though, prayed for him, he was that kind of kid. His own family moved to Mexico, I thought that'd be a good thing, to get him out of Utah, I tried, even went to court, but the judge wouldn't let him out of jail to go with them.

"He did eighteen months the last time. For stealing a motorcycle. He saw it sitting in someone's driveway, just got on it, drove it around the block to where he was staying, parked it in the driveway. Just crazy. He was busted twenty minutes later by Officer Bean, the same officer who had arrested him twice before. Bean really had it out for David Michaels. It was that eighteen months that I got close to him.

"He had so many plans for going straight, going to college. I wrote all his release recommendations. Una and I found him an apartment. But you wouldn't believe it, in five days he was busted again. Officer Bean again. Another sex offense. David was nineteen now and he'd picked up a fifteen year old runaway on the interstate. He let her stay in his apartment. They found a roach too. Well, it was all over, he was on probation. When I got him out on bail, he said he'd rather die than go back to jail. That really haunts me now. He jumped. Disappeared. Crazy kid. Why he couldn't get it together just a couple of years to straighten out his legal problems—I've seen others do it.

"He stole a car, 89 north to Logan, skirted Bear Lake, got into Wyoming, Kemmerer, ever been there? Kemmerer's an evil town. Hit 80 at Little America. Oh God he cried to me in Denver when he called the mountains so awesome he was afraid of them. He cried crazy things, like the cement ribbon he was driving in late October beneath the full moon rising. He called the highway a cement ribbon, I'll never forget that. He was a natural poet, crazy like that with his eyes. I know that area so well myself, the years I patrolled there, the Cache Mountains banked like bald giants you drive beneath feeling so dwarfed. Like animal backs, breathing. Can't you just see it? Little America! Top of the world. World's largest number of gas pumps. Sixty-five. He bought booze there at the drive-in liquor store. He said he wanted to be a trucker. He described a metallic blue and silver chrome semi with a stained-glass window in its sleeper. A rose in the sunset. But something bad happened to him he said when he was leaving Little America. A cardboard box slid in the wind across the parking lot. Right down the front of fifty, fifty, he said he counted them, fifty semis lined in a row with their engines running. When he caught up with the box, opened the door and reached down for it, all their headlights came on, flashed right on him. Like being in a police lineup, he said. So he took off. A bat out of hell. He was sure they were after him. He didn't have a map, didn't know where he was going, just stayed on the interstate, going east, a star rising in the V of the mountains in front of him. He wasn't a bad kid. Just mixed up. Crazy.

"In Rock Springs he hid a while in a dark saloon. Age limit in Wyoming is eighteen. But drinking, his paranoia got worse. He was sure they were after him. He drove down, took a look at Flaming Gorge in the moonlight, but turned back. Dams made him sick, he said, like prisons, and everywhere he looked there were park rangers. Besides, that road leads back into Utah. Then the rabbits started getting to him. In the cold you know they're attracted to the warmth of the asphalt. He said those jack rabbits sit there, on their haunches listening to the lights bearing down the highway to squash them. He wasn't going to sit on his haunches. Three stars were rising then, he said, did I see them? Or maybe they were planets. He lay in the car and remembered a book he'd read in jail about Crazy Horse. Crazy Horse was certain they were going to kill him so he took his wife off the reservation, was leading her back to her people. They were pursued by No Water and fifty Indian scouts, two hundred dollars for the man who got him. But Crazy Horse, listen to this, ran his horses down hill and then, climbing, he slowed them to a walk. Imagine that kind of nerve. No Water lost three horses trying to catch him but they never got within shooting distance even though they saw them many times, Black Shawl Woman in the lead. When he finally slept he said he dreamed of an old Mormon woman pulling her things by handcart west across the Rockies through the dying on the trail, the Nauvoo mob in close pursuit. Nauvoo was in Illinois, you know, where Joseph Smith was martyred.

"It was hard to sleep. So cold. And he was scared. He was right on the Continental Divide he learned later, a rest stop there. It's such a desert he didn't realize he was over seven thousand feet high. It's called the Red Desert there. The wind came from the south. He said he thought all night the wind was the cops after him.

"Next morning in Rawlins he finally got a map. He saw a sign on an old Indian jewelry shop. Vern Wood, Local Philosopher, Writer, Rosicrucian, Mystic. 'What do you think that guy does, Blacky?' he asked me. Darned if I knew. He seemed to be looking for role models, ideas of what he might be. He'd never seen the Pacific Ocean but he said he thought that Eastern Wyoming must be what it's like. The land coming at you in yellow waves. He was running parallel to the Snowy Range. He talked of those Arapahoe tales where the buffalo climbed to the top of the Snowy Range, then climbed out through a hole in the sky because they knew white people were coming. Everything was barren yellow but the outline of mountains, red with quaking, flaming trees. He was looking for a hole to climb out of, he said. He saw a herd of something strange, he didn't know what, sort of like deer. He described them as small and delicate, thin sticks for legs, color of the land, yellow with white spots. They were running as fast as he was. Must have been Pronghorns. A jet streaked the sky. He was afraid of the words it might spell. David, David, this is Skywriter. *I see you.* He said the snow guards lining the highway were like swords. Approaching Laramie he remembered Crazy Horse used to hang out on the plains waiting for the gate at Ft. Laramie to open. Then he would charge, yelling, whooping, naked on his horse, *naked!* except for the painted hail spots, a lightning streak down his face. He'd charge through the gate mounted backwards on his horse, race around and around inside the fort invincible to the bullets, all the soldiers shooting, and race out again, screaming bloody murder across the plains. Just to freak the pale faces. Ha!

"Sometimes he thought he was on a motorcycle racing. Other times he was driving the fastest car in the world on the Bonneville Speedway. He decided to go to Denver. He dropped down the back way, 287 behind Cheyenne. In jail he'd heard lots of good stories about Denver. That's where he could live. A crazy town for a crazy like him. There was a couple on horseback he drove along with a while, a shepherd dog leading them. He wanted a girlfriend. It wasn't fair to be busted for that girl. She was like him. He described cattle clustered under a windmill, the way the sky gathered around them, he was drunk, stoned, something, I don't know. He mentioned cowboys herding horses, weird sandstone formations appearing out of nowhere, just standing in the middle of nowhere. Maybe he could be a geologist, he said. The land he said made him think. Then everything changed, the way it does there. Pines, green mountains, cars, cities, Colorado. It freaked him. He kept dropping south, keeping the Rockies on his right. There was snow in them now. Lots of it. He rambled on and on about the Face in the Glacier, that girl frozen somewhere in the Rockies. Every few years when the glacier churns over she's lifted to view, her look so surprised, frozen right at you, her arms raised up for you to save her. He knew a lot of bizarre things like that, jail lore.

"By the time he called me from Denver he was really strung-out. It was cold and smoggy. He'd been there two days, was real down, sleeping in the car. You can imagine after Utah. Denver's a hard city. He was homesick I think. Talked about everything. Asked me if I'd heard that song *I turn to stone when you are gone*. He said Halloween was freaking him out. Indians, gypsies, spaceman in the store windows. He'd seen the real thing in Wyoming. The kid was stoned on something. *'What do you want to be when you grow up?'* He seemed angry with me. *'A cop?'* I think he forgot for a while that I am a cop. The truth is I almost forgot too. *'Trick or treat, trick or treat!'* he went on and on, *'cops and robbers, cops and robbers,'* terrible sing-song voice. He was *mimicking* me. I told him to come back. We'd work it out. I told him he didn't have a chance to be anything if he didn't. I talked him into it. Told him to come straight to our house. We were still living in Brigham City then. There was nowhere else to go. The night was all around him. I could feel it in the wires. The mountains were monsters. He was just a boy. The world was too large. He was used to being in jail. Out there, the East, Winter, broke, what is there? Who cares even if he died who would know? His place was Utah. He was drunk, stoned, running out of clean clothes. He couldn't stand that. He kept asking to talk to Una because once she had told him the stars are the Holy Ghost, Jesus is the Moon, God is the Sun. But the mystery is death, he said. 'What happens, Blacky, anyway? Do you know?' I told him I did. I'd teach him about it. So he started back.

"I think about him crossing the Rockies in the Fall. You know how beautiful they are then. That is when *I* think Jesus will return. Just before winter, He will descend the east side into the plains on his white horse. It is only in the Rockies that there'll be no Civil War. This is what we believe. The Constitution will hang by a thread. The Lamanites will rise again. The White House will burn to the ground, then be rebuilt in the Rockies by the Church. The Rockies are the holy place on Earth. It's Scripture. This is why America has been preserved until these latter days, why the Saints have come down.

"Right where 91 comes into 70—again, on the Continental Divide—he panicked, changed his mind, headed south for Leadville. Then he called me again. God it was cold. I told him to be careful. He said it again he'd rather die than go back to jail. I told him we could work it out, he'd be free of the mess in no time. Just come back. Come to our house. Una talked to him too. She told him to come by way of Aspen, to come over Mt. Elbert, the highest point in Colorado, almost fifteen thousand feet and dig the town. She told him he'd love it. We were afraid the road would be closed. But he got over. We've always wondered what he thought of that place, all those rich people. Then coming down the Roaring Fork, hitting the Colorado, coming through Rifle. In Grand Junction he stopped at his sister's. He was making a darn circle right in the middle of the country.

"The sister, Melinda Marie Edwards, twenty-two, called me while he was there. She said he had a stolen car and that he'd taken her gun. He said he was going to try to make it to our house but if they tried to stop him they'd never take him alive.

"And so he comes back into Utah. That's when I remembered I was a cop, his probation officer for Pete's sake. And now he was in the country I know best. Moab. Oh, Moab. I grew up in Montecello, Blanning. I was almost as wild as he was. A crazy Lamanite. So of course I put out an all-points bulletin for him.

"He was coming down into that desert. Coming through Green River. The Highway Patrol called me several times. Is he dangerous, or what? Oh, Dear Lord, what a night. A kid across the desert in the middle of the night with a gun. It was possible he'd use it. He was so strange, I couldn't understand him, I loved him. I was caught bet tween being his friend, his probation officer and having been a seventeen-year member of the Utah Highway Patrol. Those guys were my friends. Used to be my old patrol. Maybe I shouldn't have put out the bulletin on him. He trusted me. He was coming back on my word. But the kid needed help. He had a gun. I felt like his father who turned him in. He could never understand his father doing that to him. Una and I got down on our knees and prayed.

"He was coming through Green River. It was Hallowween night. I can see the place now. One strip through town. You can see from one end to the other. Two cafes. The street full of little demons. The UHP kept calling me. They were following him, talking to me on the phone. I was telling them the whole story, just as I'm telling you now. I could see him up ahead. It was like I was in the patrol unit, then like I was David himself, with the cops on my tail. Then they cut-off.

"They said the car slowed up, came to a halt at the side of the road. They approached cautiously. The radio was blaring. He was slumped over the wheel. He'd shot himself.

"There was the funeral. God, it was ugly. Have you ever been to a Mormon funeral? They are beautiful, meaningful. The family came up from Mexico. His brother Greg was just the opposite of David. He came to the funeral in rags, scraggly long hair, a beard, huaraches. I just couldn't understand him dressing that way for his brother's funeral. To have so little respect. No wonder the kid was messed up. Me and the father were the only ones who cried. The mother was cold. And I always thought they were close, that she loved him. I remembered she cried in the supermarket when he first got busted. The sister showed no emotion. Melinda. 'The best thing,' she said."

"You know that Beatles' tune, 'blew his mind out in a car?'"

Scorpio climbed the southern sky behind Blacky as he told me his story of David Michaels, and Sagittarius, chest out, bow drawn, riding his starry horse to the center of the galaxy. Crazy Horse must have been a Sagittarius. The light of the constellations illuminated the white rock on Timpanogos where Johnny Lookfar appeared the day after his death. I turn to stone when you are gone. It was with Johnny, a Sagittarius, a Cherokee Lamanite, that I first learned these constellations. Not far from here. In American Forks. If the religion is as they believe he's up there now preparing a new galaxy for Una, his Eternal Bride, as a bed for them to lie in. Together, then, when they love they will bring forth from their bodies new planets. Of all the subsequent life of that galaxy they will be the Gods. But who, I always wonder, is Blacky in this cosmic plan? Mormons and polygamy: the oldest problem. I agreed with him that the story of David would make a good book, a good movie as he was saying now. I saw the boy coming back into Utah to his own story. I saw my own David. Sometimes your storyline is the only line you have to Earth. And sometimes, the only line off, as I sensed Blacky felt, as carrier of David's story for which he was so responsible. A good story, but it didn't have anything to do with me. I want to write stories from the consciousness of the poet. I didn't try to explain this to Blacky. I was tired and depressed. I said goodnight, retired to Roses and Moonlight in the carport.

Morning starts at five-thirty with individual prayers. At six-fifteen, family prayers. Then the many kids troop off to seminary before regular school. I woke almost in prayer myself, *Dear God, let him call me.* Moonlight came back from a visit with a neighborhood dog in heat, flopped down under Roses and cried. She had not relieved his sorrow. He was unhappy the whole time we were in Utah. He wanted the ocean, the fog. We packed. I called Navarro, Mendocino. No one had heard from Robin. I worried about a car wreck. Should we go to Idaho? Darien said no. We took off.

But with one thing and another, shops and kids Darien needed to see, it was almost six before we got through rush traffic and started south to San Diego to my sister's. I had planned to leave by three because Roses boils over in hot weather. We had to get across the desert in one haul, at least to San Bernardino by morning, or we'd be forced to sit out a whole day. We descended south to Utah's Dixie, descended into those waving yellow seafields, the lurid flames of sunset, the rising full moon. Goodbye, David. Brother. Son. You belong to these mountains now, the desert. We rode all night at a low boil. Sometime after dark Darien climbed into the back with Moonlight and went to sleep. Now, it's just the two of us. Mother. Daughter. Midnight, a gas station in St. George as the road descends into that hot radioactive hollow: BOILING OVER? WE CAN COOL YOU. I rolled on past. I didn't have time to let them cool me. South of town I bought a six-pack. I was in Denny's on the west side of Las Vegas at two a.m. drinking coffee, swallowing No-Doz pills. A pretty young Indian boy was waiting for a waitress my age to get off work. The slot machines had the familiar Denny's orange and brown motif. On the wall next to me was a framed burlap display of a "choni," which, it was explained, "is the Yaqui scalp of an Apache." The black hair was braided with a red bow on a round piece of dried skin. *Used for strangling sleeping people and for herding cattle, especially rustling. Black magic,* it summed up. At the gas station the attendant was thrilled by the RV at the pumps next to me. It was the largest single sale of gasoline he'd ever made. An hour later I was well into California. A half-hour beyond that I could go no further. It was the lowest, dreariest part of the desert. The air was suffocating. I pulled off at a rest stop, found a place in the long line of cars, my lights flashing across various parts of their sleeping occupants. The sudden intimacy was disturbing. On the chainlink fence along which the cars were parked were continuous signs WARNING! DO NOT DRINK THE WATER! WARNING DO NOT DRINK THE WATER! WARNING . . . . I put Moonlight in the front, climbed into the back and lay down beside the longlimbed aircooled sleeping body of my daughter. I had to rest but I couldn't fall so deep away that I'd forget where I was or how much time had passed. I figured I could sleep fifteen minutes. The passing semis felt like planes hitting the landing strip. The curtain kept blowing across my face a flame of searing light. The landscape turned in circles, the car coming slowly to a halt at the side of the road. The boy ran out for the pass, the clouds turning to roses beneath the purple mountains. His mother was crying. Her son's perfect hands reached into the Wasatch for the ball. The full moon came up in them when No Water appeared at the window. Her screams tumbled as radioactive floodwater down the canyon. Through the hole in the sky the couple placed a rag over her nose and mouth. Then the car screeched spun. Slammed into the wall just as the boy carrying a violin case made-it across the Canadian border. I woke. The tonnage of highway lay on top of me. I turned to stone to hold back the moan so as not to wake my daughter.

LULU IN BRAZIL

I fled the movie. I fled the city. I crossed the Golden Gate doing 75. I dropped down off the freeway into Sausalito. I needed a drink. The 150 mile drive ahead of me, the night mountain road to Mendocino, was not going to be easy.

Zack's. Walk in. A three-piece copy band, loud and clangy. Find a seat in the furthest corner. Avoid being hassled. Let go your anger, meditate on the Bay, the neon rainbow lights floating the calm water. A gull flapping out over his reflection. With much ado he sits down on the dark mirror, before a razor line of diminishing yacht prows. *Lulu*. And my old friend Jewel as Jack the Ripper. Every time I encountered him in the past few weeks he had urged me to go to the city and see him play Jack the Ripper in the movie *Lulu*. I knew he was somewhere in the audience. I fled up the aisles through what seemed, as the lights came on, an endless sea of sneering gay men. I raced through the crowded lobby, eyes averted to the crimson carpet, afraid I'd see him. I fled through the crimson blood, rivers of her gushing onto his face, the familiar maniacal lust of an old lover's eyes. How much delight the film takes in its final revenge on her. How much delight he took slicing her, with the butcher knife hidden in his black overcoat. From the cunt all the way up.

A young man is staring at me. Fuck. His ghost-white face comes to me from across the room. Black hair oiled close to a small head. He stares at me blatantly, absurdly. I ignore him, turn my seat as far north as it will go, sip my wine, trying not to see the images of *Lulu*. Daddy calls me *Lulu*. He always has. The man is moving to the table opposite me. He stares. And stares. Preposterously. But the wine is working, the screaming going out of me. It's not possible to ignore him. I snicker, sort of. He takes the acknowledgement as an invitation, gets up and sits down at my table. You are beautiful. I must know who you are.

He gets right into it, accusing me of all the things I've always been accused of. Why aren't you smiling? Are you mad? You should be smiling. Do you want to forget? I can help you to forget. Are you sad? Do you think of yourself as better than everyone here? You know, there are people who put up barry-airs—his accent is on the last syllable and I don't understand—barry-airs, he repeats the word for me several times—people who put up barry-airs that you can't get around. Where are you from? Brazil. But he has barry-airs himself, answering my questions with reluctance. Yes. I grew up in Rio de Janeiro. I'm in the shipping business. But let's talk about you. You are beautiful. I must know you.

His face is small, his body like a delicate hummingbird. The slick black hair is a startling contrast to the white skin like porcelain. A 40s matinee idol on a small black and white screen. I'm large, my heaviest, much larger than he, months at the typewriter trying to finish my book. Though he offers to help me, I don't remove my red-plaid wool jacket. I'm wearing faded levis, scuffy boots. Images from *Lulu* keep asserting themselves across my vision. Soon there is another glass of wine before me. He drinks Jamaican rum. You seem like a woman who has put it all down. I can't tell if you're from the country or the city. You seem like a city woman who doesn't care anymore. Who's seen too much. You don't care about people.

I watch the dancers, the musicians who take breaks after every tune. I care about people. I watch the cocktail waitress. I care about your blond hair. I watch a middle-aged couple talking intensely at the fire. The man is black, the woman very fat, about fifty. She seems happy, elated. When she rises and walks across the dance floor to the women's room I see that she is white. Do you condescend to poor people? Again, his accent, the meaning of his question is difficult to decipher. Condescend? *Condescend.* I laugh a little in understanding, I'm *descended* from poor people. Are you married. No. Silence. Do you like me? Sure.

I'm still having a hard time to understand the American woman. My father is very rich, is Admiral in the Brazilian Navy. I was raised in the city, Rio, and in the country. I was raised everywhere. But that is nothing. Please tell me your name. I must know what you are. Do you work? Please tell me where you work.

I tell him that I'm a poet. I work everywhere. He reaches for my notebook. May I write in it? Sure. He writes several rhymed couplets, the kind men offer when you tell them you are a poet, to show you that they too are sensitive souls. The night is down/but you are the dawn. He catches my eyes and says with passionate insistence I want to know who you are! I look back into his eyes and smile, very gently, I bet you don't.

A long silence. The rock n roll fills the room. A note arrives from four cowboys sitting across from us. An address in Idaho. I laugh. I can't help it. I love Idaho. Laughter from their table in response to mine. My name is Lu. Lulu? No. And yours? I ask him several times before he writes it in my notebook. Tomas de Albiom. Tom. It's Portuguese. Why do you want to know, you are beautiful. I just read a book about the history of the Portuguese in California. I'm very rich. I'm in the shipping business. But that's not important. I must see you again. But you have barry-airs. I'm thinking about Idaho. Where Monroe sang River Of No Return and Chief Joseph led the Nez Perce in the infamous retreat. I've been writing a poem for months about Idaho. He is telling me a story. I listen as I watch another gull waltz her water reflection

My grandfather went into the jungles of Brazil in the Thirties. His mission was to contact the Indians living south of the Amazon. He cleared an area. It took him two years of sending in gifts to the Indians before they trusted him.

I look at him. Then what happened? Oh, that's not important. That's too heavy. My grandfather, he's still alive. He is very rich. I just tell you this story to illustrate a point about you. You are a person with barry-airs. You make me feel like my grandfather camped around the Indians who don't trust him.

I look at him. What happened to the Indians? You're too heavy. My sweetest laugh. You think too much. You should be light. You should be gay. Then you would be beautiful. Why don't you let me take you home?

I'm lost again in the room. Idaho. I don't want to die, Joseph declared, in a strange land. The cowboys drink to me. I nod my head, toast them back. How do you spend your days? I mean, what do you do when you get up? To tell him is cruel. He asks again. I'm a writer. I get up and I sit down and I start writing.

There is a long silence. Three minutes maybe. I watch the dancers. The black man and fat white woman hold each other close. It occurs to me that they were married today and this is their honeymoon.

I liked you better as a woman.

I laugh. I can't help it. The wine has improved my disposition immensely. You haven't liked anything about me that I've shared, which is the reason, of course, for my barriers. Give me another chance. Can I see you? I live far away. That makes no difference. I will come to see you. You are beautiful. My attention wanders. I watch the dancers. Jack the Ripper, Grandpa. Slashing through the jungle.

He becomes more resourceful as we spin into the final reel. If I lived next door to you in your town would you see me? My delight erupts in a genuine *ha*! I think about it. I write out my address. I rise from the table and hand it to him. I pick up my notebook, swallow the last of my wine. I look at him seeing the long road home. Well, you know. Anything is possible. To begin with you'd have to tell me what your grandpa did to the Indians.

SLEEPING LADY

I can't stop crying. I don't know why. We come out of the bar and it is he who is crazy. He has always claimed this special privilege in our relationship. He loves me because I am so sane, so nice, so understanding and forgiving of his craziness. I hardly realize when the tears begin, when the sobbing becomes the same as my breathing.

◇ ◇ ◇

We hitched down from Mendocino for my poetry reading. By saving the $50 gas money I would be able to make five copies of my manuscript. We hitched too because I wanted to be on the road with him again. But it was like coming out of three months in solitary confinement. The August light was blinding. I was ten pounds overweight from sitting ten-twelve hours a day at the typewriter. I went back twice to change my clothes: everything was too tight. Three blocks from the cottage, up on the highway, he went, without warning, into one of his fits. He fled up the wooded hill, tearing the pack from his back. He had been making the pack all summer while I typed the final manuscript, the mountain backpack being a symbol he kept saying of what he would do next with his life. Through the trees I saw him rip the denim I had taken time out to sew for him. Then he banged the carefully measured, sanded, nailed and polished frame against the jagged wire edge of the highway fence, then threw the whole thing into the redwoods. I was running up the hill after him, calling his name, noting that as always he had the presence of mind not to harm his violin, when I just stopped, turned back to the highway. Fuck it. Fuck him. I was crossing the highway when he emerged from the woods, still frantic and running, mumbling some shit about how much he loved me. I went into a rare rage. *You don't! You'd have more consideration for me!* He acted startled, surprised. He seemed to say you're right. If I loved you I'd have more consideration for you. We were staring at each other in epiphanic recognition when I became aware of the gaping occupants of the cars whizzing past. One car was stopped for us.

Someone picked us up, took us down the coast to the Navarro River, the junction of Highway I and I28. They gave us a joint which he smoked, calming him. He always said it was finding marijuana ten years before that humanized him, that saved him from insanity. His drug therapy. I believed him. We waited two hours over the deliquescent river mouth and beach, beneath the bluffs, the poet entertaining the bored musician. I can still be charming and funny, I can still make him laugh. When I put my hand on the bulge between his legs, he said, "Oh god. I'll never find another woman as brilliant as you."

Cars kept passing, speeding up when they saw us. Bastards, he cursed. What do we look like, I wondered, moving down the highway to look back at the couple, as I imagined them. A blue heron in the water behind them, Navarro Head above them. Musicians, I decided. I grew worried that we wouldn't make my reading in Mill Valley by eight. He said if we didn't get a ride in another half hour he'd hitch down the coast to Elk, an easy ride to get—the problem was hitching inland—and borrow a friend's car. Instead, we were picked up by a young couple in a Volkswagon who lived on the Sacramento River in a houseboat and were pissed the whole three-hour drive to the city about the boat people coming to this country taking all the jobs and living spaces. Robin whispered to me, "I guess they mean boats." In the cramped backseat of this car we got very stoned.

I read at the Mill Valley Bus and Book Depot with a poet named Alvin, a "surrealist," the series coordinator had said on the phone, and a librarian at U.C. Berkeley, newly from New York. Typical of his geography's ethic he read with disdain for his own work, for his audience, and particularly, it seemed, for me. I, on the other hand, typical of my California, was overly nice. It happens every time I read first, which I volunteered to do to be nice. I was concerned the whole time about taking up his time. I read for twenty minutes, time enough only for the LA Blonde poems and one of the *Tales of Talmapais*, "Sleeping Lady," a poem to the reclining figure who shapes Mt. Talmapais above Mill Valley. *Enemies lied to her, said her warrior was killed in battle. So she pines away.* Greyhound buses kept arriving and departing in the open door behind me. The exhaust and engine noise and people loading with their things were distracting. Robin kept flitting from one corner to another, quailing behind the walls of books like a caged bird. The audience was like stone. Unresponsive, polished, expensive pet stones. Jaded, stoned probably, and like me, female: overly nice, yet in the most passive manner, daring me to turn them on. I failed. Miserably. Alvin read his surrealism for over an hour and they seemed to love him, especially his disdain for them.

Later, at the Old Mill Bar, after a couple of beers, I approached the surrealist. He looked up at me with a loathing that again startled me, forcing me to explain my approach. "I just wanted to connect with you before this is all over." "Well," he sneered, "connect." Robin, fiddle in tow, was flinging himself from bar to dartboard and back against the bay window, dashing out to the midnight street, returning in an even worse frenzy. Embarrassed by my poor reading and now by him, I pretended he wasn't doing this. In the beginning our love was all in supporting each other in our arts, our terrifying and lonely endeavors. Now he couldn't tolerate a single reading. I thought of the countless evenings I had spent with his non-verbal, doped musician friends, how I enjoyed them, how privileged and honored I felt to share his world. Alvin was saying "I hate confessional poetry. I'd never write a poem about my wife." I looked down at him and said, "I'm sure you wouldn't. Men don't. They write about what's important to them."

Darcy, a good friend and sister poet, invited us to spend the night at her house, three blocks away. I said no, we want to sleep outdoors. Becoming concerned she said we could sleep on her deck beneath the redwoods. I hugged her and said no, we have to get away. We need to be alone, we need some raw, real experience with the world. Something new.

◇ ◇ ◇

We have come out of the bar with our things, his violin, my manuscript in the Navaho bag, our sleeping bags. I take hold of his arm. We walk north away from Throckmorton, away from the street light. At the corner we turn west, head up the back street. "Let's find a *beautful* place to sleep." "I hate poets," he answers. I begin to cry. "Well," he mimes the surrealist, "connect." The gush of water from my eyes is a surprise. And uncontrollable. *I'm crying!* We are limping, holding onto each other, holding each other up, down a dark redwood-lined street of Mill Valley and I am crying. The tears won't stop, this hasn't happened in years, they seem to be spouting from an unknown source. I never cry. It is so surprising I'm laughing through the streaming downpour on my face.

We come to the city park. It is extremely dark, the echoing deep still darkness of redwood forests. *Forbidden places to the Indians. The Se-kah who dwell here can make people crazy.* We stumble, me crying, toward the center, to a large round of redwoods. I stand in it while he wanders away. My tears water the trees. Over my sobs I can hear the soft cascading of a creek. When a redwood is cut, a circle of new trees springs up from the stump that remains. This is the largest circle of redwoods I have ever seen, though these rounds grow all over the scarred land of Northern California, perfect cathedral circles of baby giants surviving the slaughter of their parents. "It must have been cut twice," I sob. "First, the virgin tree, then the round of second growth." Tears drop from my nose onto the soft-packed dirt as I walk the circle. "No," he answers, quieter now. "These trees are a hundred years old. They must have grown from one tree."

We look across the wide shadowy floor. For all our love of the big trees, our seeking them out, our poetry and music to them, redwood surely being our history, our love, we can hardly believe this is the base of a single tree. There is no discussion. This is the place we will sleep.

He spreads out the sleeping bags. I hold my Navaho bag against myself, quietly mindlessly sobbing. I intend to stuff it with my wallet, $50 plus the $15 I earned from the reading, down into my sleeping bag, a precaution against theft. Then I think to use it as a pillow. Then I have a strange thought. *Let the thief have it.* Wiser to put the bag away from me. Foolish to endanger myself for $65, for even the manuscript. I notice that Robin has propped his violin against the legs of the redwood picnic table twenty feet away. I prop my Navaho bag next to his violin. When I wonder about my lack of concern for my uncopied book more tears rush from my eyes.

On the rooty floor beneath the enormous redwoods, within the perfect circle, the moon moving into the betrayer of my heart, Leo, I sob. I lie on my back next to him, in my separate bag, and I can't stop crying. The trees reach as a spiralling wall from our wide rootbed hundreds of feet to a small skylight through which the stars are shooting. And I cry. And cry. After a long while he realizes I am crying. He forgets for a moment his own pain, takes me in his arms. "One? What's wrong, One?" I don't know. I can't say. It is buried too deep like the roots of these trees, springing from an unknown virgin cut. "We're cut off from each other." I sob for my unreachable roots. I sob for the bed of Ulysses and Penelope, how they recognized each other twenty years later only through the secret they shared, their nuptial bed in a tree stump. I sob for the preparation of the cut, the equipment, the blades, the ropes, the men, the semen I always smell when I think of the old loggers, the nice liberals of Mill Valley who let this happen. I can hear the cutting. It is a song like the sound of his violin, his ax, he always calls it. The floor like blood beneath us, deep, alive to the massacre, the roots' struggle against the slaughter, the hacking, their growing consciousness, what they have to do to survive. *There is no natural death for redwood.* They have to be killed. "Imagine," I sob into his white meaty shoulders and laugh through the wracks, quoting my long-ago lover, Maximillian, "men with balls enough to cut down a tree this size." I am drunk, I am dead, my tears water the trees. *In the beginning there was only water and only the tips of Tamalpais stood above the water.* He holds me until he falls asleep. I hear the saws at work, the whining, crying, screeching song of his ax.

I lie very still for a long time in the heart of the earth. Silence. Exhaustion. As if we are growing from the ground, these holy trees from decimation, dishonor, the meaning of the crucifixion. Our bones fall through the earth, his sleep with its deep, even breathing. Such a sleeper he is for one so crazed when awake. Pluto, my man, my Orpheus. While I, so reasonable awake, can never sleep. What am I afraid of? Eurydice dropped at the last moment, falling back to the Underworld. In the moment of sleep I am the root springing up, *anything* for air, for light, for survival.

I dream of a boy to whom I am fatally attached. Our relationship is this fact. Nothing more. We are in relationship. We face each other, in semi-foetal positions, our legs gathered to our chests, the union of our two halfs making a circle. We converse. What we say to each other is what we have always said to each other. We are in a house on a hill surrounded by enormous boulders. I have been here before. I see that he wants to kill me. Now he is chasing me, I'm running for my life down the boulder-strewn treeless hill. Now he becomes a crowd chasing me. They have stolen my clothes and I run naked and ashamed, searching for cover. From the crowd he emerges again with a chainsaw. I hide behind a boulder and watch the crowd run past, the intent to kill me carrying them up the next hill and over. All the land is blue. Cold and naked, I notice a small boy's blue jacket lying across the rock. It will hide some of my nakedness, give me some warmth, protection.

I'm awakened from the dream by a dog who has been let out of his house in the early dawn and has come over to investigate the two people sleeping here. The jingle of his tag and chain as he sniffs around my head awakens me. I don't open my eyes, but from the dream to waking I wait to see what he will do. I hope he doesn't piss on me. Now he moves away to investigate Robin. Now there are two dogs. They sniff around, wander over to the violin and Navaho bag propped under the picnic table. I just know they are pissing on them.

I fall deeper asleep. Finally, after months, I am sleeeping very soundly. Tamalpais, her name is Sleeping Lady. I wake only when the dog returns. This time he steps on me with all four paws, three on my upper chest and one on my face, his chain jangling all around my head. With great force, my eyes shut tight, I shove the dog away, shouting GO AWAY! I burrow deeper into my bag, covering my head. I fall away from sound into the dark, forgetting everything. It is a sleep unlike any I have had in months, maybe years.

When I wake Robin is already up, gone. I look for him through the trees searching too for a place to pee. There is a man on the edge of the creek watching me. When Robin and I come together through the expanse of grass and trees we are lovers again. We smile, touch each other affectionately. "Let's have a huge breakfast. Whatever we want," I say. It is so unusual for us to have money. I look into the eyes of the man who is watching us from the other side of the creek. We walk into the village, sun and morning and morning people on the street. *Robin, I love you. I watch you from across the red streetlight that catches me and you are beautiful.* But then I see that the man from the park is standing near him in the crowd. We find a deli, a table. I reach for my wallet in the Navaho bag. It is gone.

It is so like him to be saying, "you stay here, I'll go back." He knows how badly I need my morning coffee. He goes back to the bar, the last place I remember seeing it. The janitor hasn't seen it. He retraces our steps, our crying stumbling steps of the night before, back to the circle of redwoods. I think it must have dropped out of my too full bag on that back street. He is gone for a long time. I have coffee with the loose change in my levis.

Robin returns, showing his empty hands to me from the door. I buy him a cup of coffee with the last of my change. We start back to the park, hungry, our things heavy. I see over and over the sobbing steps, the path of the night before, the dog who was really the thief, *he placed his hands on me, no wonder I fell asleep,* but how I woke in the morning to sun shafting through the towering redwoods, how glad I was to be alive, *I had that very thought,* how much joy I felt when I looked to his violin and my Navaho bag unmolested, or so it seemed, beneath the picnic table, so beautiful their coupling. On the outer edge of the redwood circle I find a boy's blue jacket draped over a rock. I don't touch it. We find my wallet in the shallows of the creek, its insides pulled and thrown. Photos of my children, my football player floating, my daughter caught in the rocks, smiling through her long hair, my own face on the California license in a drowned eucalyptus branch. He steps right into the flowing creek, so like him, new sneakers, socks and pants, and retrieves my girl, my boy, my identification.

We borrow $50 from Darcy. We walk back through the streets of Mill Valley. Fog is painting the face of Tamalpais. *Fog! Pelican is beating your wife!* We go to the Bus and Book Depot, take the bus to Berkeley through San Francisco. Out on the highway I look at Mt. Tamalpais, the fog at once ethereal and a cold fact. The summit is obscured, then reappears as a woman asleep, victim of lost love and inaccurate information. The origin of the name is obscure. Some say *mal pais,* bad lands. The Miwok say the summit is forbidden, you can't go to the top and survive. The Rock Giant will devour you.

All afternoon we work together in the hot copy center. He takes over with his quick hands when I flounder with the machine. I take over when he doesn't understand the order of pages. Mostly we work in unison and as always this is thrilling. Afterwards he takes me to a place on Shattuck for Happy Hour. But the drinks are expensive and they no longer serve hors d'oeuvres as he had remembered, the free meal we were hoping for. We are hungry, dirty, tired, depressed, broke, in debt. I am fat, my clothes faded, ragged. He is coming back through the pretty, high-fashioned city crowd from the bathroom and I realize he has masturbated. "Well, I couldn't take it any longer. The cocktail waitress." I look at her, young, with lots of make-up, but not very sexual, it seems to me, and I realize how bad things are between us. Why didn't we make love last night under the redwoods? This has never happened to me before. No matter how bad things get between me and my man the sex is always good. I can't bring myself to admit I don't enjoy fucking him. There, I've said it. I hear the friend's words that have haunted me all summer, how she finally left her husband. "It just got so I couldn't fuck him anymore."

Then we see the headlines of the *Examiner*. WOMAN RAPED, KILLED CLIMBING MT. TAM. August 20, 1979. I feel the dog at my throat, I see the man's eyes, I think of surrealism, confessionalism, the great cathedral round of redwoods. Survivors.

II
Searching For Psyche

THE BLUES

or, *Are you Up Here By Yourself Or With An Old Man?*

You get off work. You lied and bluffed to get the job, checked out a book on it from the library. *Wing it,* a poet said to you, who owns a bar herself and so you have been winging it, seeing her eyes in every drink you don't know how to mix. Now you don't know what to do with your time off. You walk home. You walk up the steep steps of the bluff to Uptown. You live Uptown. You work Downtown. On Water Street. You've chosen this town because three of its sides are water, one of those is a foreign country, its populace is full of poets, and the mayor is a jazz pianist. You let the dog out for a minute, sit on the porch while he runs around frantically, telling him he'll have to wait for his walk. He's never been locked up in his life. Mt. Baker puffs on the horizon. But you have to lie down. You climb the stairs again to the second floor. You lie down. You feel a man on top of you. His hands touch your face. You can see him. Feel his great entrance. You love him so much you are crying. You pick up *Playgirl.* You drop that, pick up *Delta of Venus: Erotica.* The author wrote this book for a rich male patron she hated, "caricaturing sexuality." Now the book is famous. You feel this woman always wrote for that man. You can't sleep. You get up, take your second bath of the day. In your last place there was no plumbing. You start to touch yourself, want to, but know you'll cry and the water is so hot you're afraid you'll pass out. You need your strength to walk the dog. *O.K., Moonlight!* as you climb out of the tub. He yelps, jumps, lands both fleshy paws, first one, then the other, delicately on your breasts. You dress, go down the stairs. You've been worrying about this walk for an hour, where to walk, how much strength do you have? You are so tired. So you get into your car *Roses*. (How strange to look out the window and see her parked here, the long blue silvery Straits, Whidbey Island, gigantic volcanic Mt. Baker puffing behind her.) You want him to run around until Roses warms up. But he's worried too. Here we are all alone in this strange place. He cries so you let him in. He scrambles over your shoulder. Sometime, somehow in the drive up here the handle to the backdoor disappeared. Now she has three broken doors. You woke this Sunday morning to a radio sermon about the doors of opportunity standing so wide open they're falling off their hinges. Just as the preacher said, you're afraid of them. The broken hinges, that is. You drive down to the Town Tavern, let Moonlight out to run Water Street with the other dogs, buy a glass of burgundy. Grapes grown thirty miles from the home you have fled. Happy Hour entertainment. A young woman singing *The Blues*. Her name is Eva Ditrichson and she sounds exactly like old Jimmy Reed. You can't help but think that's absurd. You wonder about integrity. Then, when he asks, you lie for the first time in your life about your age. Not because you want him to think you are younger but because you are too lonely and tired to deal with fear in his eyes. You consider which four years of your life you'd like to forget. All week the boys born the year your son was have been registering for the draft. This morning before work, in front of the post office, with a poet you have read for years and now meet on this day, her birthday, you talked a boy out of registering. "My husband came back from Viet Nam insane," she said to the boy. "My son is your age," you said to him. When you looked into his extraordinary face you remembered the day he was born and you remembered you must not beg him to make love to you. He gasps. "I can't believe you are older than me." You look at his bald head, his pinched, lined face and withered body and are afraid to ask. "26," he volunteers, shrugging his shoulders. Then he tells you he scales trees for a living and in the same breath asks you if you would like to spend the week in La Conner. You have to ask where La Conner is. Is it an island? You'd almost go. A man shooting pool bends to the table inches from the bar stool you sit on, the man next to you awaiting your answer as you remove the levis from his hips and ass. Then he asks you, while the female impersonator sings The Blues about how deep the Mississippi River is, "Do you live here?" and you tell him what you have told everyone who has asked, enjoying your answer, knowing that very soon your answer will be a simple *yes.* "Yes, I live here. I've lived here a week, two weeks, three weeks today. I got a job. I got an apartment. I got books from the library. I got a parking ticket. Guess I'm here." You don't say the other part "and soon I hope I'll have a lover." Instead, you say, "I don't understand why I am so tired." He says, this man who judges trees, "it's probably the change." You think about it. Then you want to go to La Conner with him, where ever it is, you are so grateful for his wisdom. "You are so tough, so hard on yourself," you hear again your last lover's words to you. It is then that he asks you the question, "Are you up here by yourself or are you with an old man?" You feel your tired ancient woman's face come close to forming a sneer.

All day they come in by themselves, together, the lonely people. On the first day a man and his mother celebrated his 30th birthday. They sat and drank as the tide went out and came back in, telling each other. On the second day you turned from watching a woman hang diapers from the rigging of her sailboat while a man played with two babies on deck to find that you were surrounded by men all your father's age, all of them talking about World War II. On the third day, still morning, you turned from watching the ferry bringing tourists, to the only customer, Caroline, a glamorous woman in her sixties, who was telling you of her little girl. As you poured her second Bloody Mary a tear rolled down her face. Her little girl was 35, retarded, the most beautiful person you will ever meet, who in the past three months had lost forty pounds. She was on her way to Seattle from the West End to learn the results of the tests. "They think it's her liver, I don't know what I'll do if I lose her." On the fourth day a woman said, "Oh! *You!* I saw you dancing alone at the

Judge's Chambers. It was like watching a wild young horse, the way you tossed your hair around." On the fifth day you served a famous poet secretly celebrating his 54th birthday. All day he bought the drinks of anyone sitting near him. On the sixth day four Canadian Naval Mine Sweepers docked out your window, in just the way bikers line their machines outside of bars, in just the way cowboys tie their horses to the saloon.

The sun has set but you drive to the beach before it is dark. You let Moonlight out to run. North Beach. The first place you knew here. You witnessed a drowning here. A boat capsized, one man did not make it back to shore. Now you return as if to a loved one's grave. The wind blows from the east. It ripples a long ribbon of gulls sitting on the water. You still don't know what the wind from the east means. You haven't begun to think about the volcano which has been erupting south of you all week. You remember your last dream at home: the cabin fell on top of you. Now you look across to Canada, the Cascades, west to the Olympics. The beauty is like your sexuality: suddenly, in this new place, so unknown. The smells are like home. The colors make you remember the epitaph your second love wrote: *He Was In It For The Colors*. You know you will have arrived when you have taken this place, this new lover into your body so deeply it is the landscape of your dreams.

You make your way home in the dark. You lie down. You look again at the men in *PlayGirl*. Only one is beautiful to you. You consider putting him on the wall and realize it would intimidate any man you might bring home. Then you hear the woman's amazing sounds coming from the apartment next door. You try not to listen. You are listening to sounds that come from such a foreign place you can't believe it's the sweet poet next door. The answer comes to the question most often asked you: How is it you look so young? Because you have always had a lover. You will die now, wither up and die now without one, those sounds too close to the source of life to overhear like this. You remember that for the first time in years you have been dreaming of your husband, the man who quit talking to you the night you were married.

You have left the place you love. Now you are here. You write home on the back of silver postcards of the erupting volcano, this is a photograph of my soul. You write I am very lonely. But not depressed. Here in this new place, alone, without my friends, my children, my love to share these stories and images I have learned the great difference between depression and loneliness. In depression there is no energy. In loneliness there is sorrow, but also, a kind of beauty. And in beauty there is always energy. Which must be the true, integral nature of The Blues: this open door, this entrance, this prayer for love and sleep and the coming of the land as the place of your dreams. As you fall away you hear the mayor playing the piano somewhere over the town, Uptown, Downtown, Water Street, over the Northwest corner of the country, see a solitary dancer, like a wild young horse, keeping time.

SEARCHING FOR PSYCHE

I ran into Sambo's for a cup of coffee to go. We were van hunting. Patrick called from the driver's window, "Could you get me some french fries?" We had been talking the night before in my sister's kitchen about the Irish being potato eaters. Bridgit told us of a new successful therapy for early cancer: feeding patients the food their genetic ancestors ate. We both had a craving for potatoes.

Lunch hour. Only one waitress and she was swamped. I sat on the stool next to the cash register and she asked for my order. She didn't write it down and the whole time I sat there I wasn't sure that she had it. I was anxious because we had borrowed Bridgit's car and we had to have it back to her in Ashland by six. But how bothersome my little order at lunch time. She was a short, bulging woman in her mid-fifties, with varicose veins and a brown bouffant wig. Despite her rather ignominous situation, her short, brown and orange Sambo's uniform pulled too tightly across her lumpy hips, she seemed capable, sensitive, completely in control.

I noticed a couple opposite each other at a front window table. She also was in her mid-fifties. He looked about eighteen. Against busy Highway 99 they shared the identical profile: a long delicate nose, high narrow cheekbones, a soft round forehead. He had sunbleached blond hair that fell around his shoulders in a stringy curl. Hers was the same length, but dyed a dull brown and combed straight off her forehead suggesting a 40s pompadour, a leftover of the old style rather than a fashionable re-do of it, as a girl the boy's age might wear. He was dressed in a white t-shirt, loose ragged levis. She was dressed drably, in the color of her thin hair. They were both tall, their long legs folded beneath the table in the identical manner, their long arms propped on their elbows, palms and fingers folded around their faces.

Their manner seemed as lovers, and later, Patrick suggested this. On our trip we had encountered two such relationships, of women in their fifties with men in their twenties. But probably she was his mother, or aunt, or even his grandmother. He looked like any punk kid you see anywhere, except he was sitting in a busy coffee shop drinking coffee with an older woman, to whom he was fully, exceptionally, attentive. As she was of him. She was talking to him. Occasionally she smiled wistfully. Then she would seem to share a humorous, or philosophical anecdote, a story about someone they shared. Then they smoked. She held out the package to him. He took a cigarette, put it in his mouth. She lit it for him, then the one she had put to her own mouth. Their calm seemed from profound revery though I noticed that she rubbed her crossed foot, very slightly, against the center pole of the table.

To understand their intimacy, I imagined that his father or grandfather had died, or was dying in a near-by hospital. Her husband or father. When I thought of this and looked again at them, I was certain that the man they shared was not dead yet. There wasn't the shock, the terrible hole of grief and loss. But something was happening to them. I imagined the doctors had just informed them that the disease was terminal and this is what made this boy so responsive to this older woman.

Waiting, still not sure if my order was in, I went out to get a Medford paper for the want-ads. The machine took my quarter but didn't open. I waved at Patrick still waiting behind Bridgit's wheel and moved back toward the glass front door. Through the window the boy's eyes met mine. How to describe that look? His being was open to me. His look was not of sorrow or grief or fear or joy or excitement or love or sex or petition or even of intensity as one normally thinks of that state. It wasn't resignation, it wasn't wonder. It was, very simply, openness. He was open to me as he looked at me, as he was open to her. As he seemed open to everyone in the room, the workers on their lunch break, the foolishly dressed, overworked waitress. His open look was too intimate for me. I looked away. And regretted it instantly. Such a rare opportunity, to look into an opened face, to be seen by it.

When I sat back on my stool by the cash register the waitress was putting the lid on a paper coffee cup. She called through the window to the man in the cook's hat moving up and down the grill. "Carl!" Can you give me an order of fries to go?" On the way out I noticed the want-ads of the Medford paper lying on top of the cigarette machine. I grabbed them.

That evening, racing back down I-5 from Merlin, Oregon, far too north of Ashland to get the car back by six legally, I told Patrick of the couple in Sambo's. We had just encountered another disturbing relationship, a couple newly moved from Manhattan Beach in Southern California where the father of my children lives, the town they visit often now that they are grown, who had a metallic-gold, souped-up surfer van for sale—a trick van they're also called. On the phone the woman had encouraged us to come all the way from Medford. "My husband says the first person here with cash can have it." She said she drove to Medford yesterday from Merlin and it took her twenty minutes. It took us almost an hour. The husband arrived home just as I was starting the vehicle to test drive it. He appeared suddenly between the white picket fence with a GUARD DOG ON DUTY sign and the gold house next to the Hideaway Restaurant on the mountain road to Galice and Wolf Creek, holding back a growling German Shepherd. The man, like the dog, was seething. He was enormous in a blue and black plaid flannel shirt as he told her the van was sold, "And you know it!" I saw him, as if it was happening before my eyes, slug her in the mouth. She cringed and huddled around her own body like a child rather than the forty-year-old woman she must have been. Even so, he told us to go ahead and take it for the drive. It was confusing. The woman's twenty-one-year-old son rode along with us as I eased the huge metallic-gold thing through the metallic-fall-colored mountains. If I could buy it, and I wanted to, despite Patrick's dismay—"It will ruin your image"—I knew I'd name him Merlin, getting me in touch, finally, with my Northern European heritage. "Oh, my mom," the blond surfer—who looked a lot like the boy in Sambo's—yelled from the bed in the back over the surging guitars of the sound system. "You should never listen to her. Everyone knows she's senile."

And so now, coming back down Oregon in the intimacy of the new night and long road I felt moved to describe to Patrick as he drove, what I had experienced of the boy and older woman in Sambo's. I had felt the urge to do so all day but they had seemed so beside the point, so unrelated to anything, our long fruitless search for the van my parents wanted to buy me. The van I would name Psyche.

"You mean the boy sitting in the front window?" He had noticed him too. When I was through he was quiet and then he said, "Can you capture what you just described in a single paragraph? I mean, close down a little, not go into all the things you usually do?"

EL NIÑO DEL SALVADOR: A LOVE STORY

Sometimes I live in the country,
Sometimes I live in the town.
Sometimes I get a great notion
To jump in the river and drown

"Goodnight Irene"
by Hugh Ledbetter and John Lomox

High tide.

Two pelicans perch with the gulls on the railing right out my window. A couple with a baby are handfeeding the huge, prehistoric creatures. I don't think I've ever been this close to pelicans. They're so tame. *Pelicans have become a common sight in the Wakonda Auga area in this strange summer of 1983,* the bulletin board says beneath a photo of two on the river, *having arrived on El Niño, the warm current from South America that's ruining the fishing season for the entire Northwest.* Now it's November and the board is dominated with the disasters of El Niño. Barracuda in the Straits of Juan de Fuca, sharks off the coast of Oregon, the wettest year on record in Southern Oregon. *The National Weather Service attributes the record precipitation and recent volcanic eruptions in Washington and Mexico to the El Niño effect.*

Left Psyche at the garage. Which means I've decided to let Joey go with me to Minneapolis. His money to fix her. Will I be able to stand it? Two thousand miles and back. Will I ever get over Patrick? And now Bill. As if things weren't complicated enough.

3:20. The sun burns everything. Burns my face, my breasts and shoulders. Feels good, a reprieve from all the rain. *Burn off my blues, Sun, give me back my faith.* The pelican's entire front opens to the proffered french fry. *A pelican in her piety, an emblem of Jesus Christ, a symbol of charity.* Whose line is that? I should have ordered a cup of soup. This bowl's too much.

A shadow. A cooling. A figure hovering between me and the sun.

"Can you tell me where Grenada is?"

I look up into the face of the young black man.

He says Grenada with the Spanish *a*. We invaded two weeks ago. I draw the map on my place mat. Here's Florida, Cuba, Jamaica, the West Indies come down like this, over here is the Gulf of Mexico, Central America. Grenada is right here, a little north of Venezuela. It's only six miles by eight. Did you know that?

He's wearing a silky, slightly wrinkled, pale blue dress shirt with white pin stripes. I hear the accent.

"Where are you from?"

"El Salvador."

I rise. "Please sit down."

When he does the sun is full again in my face. I feel exposed to him.

"Are you here legally?"

"No."

He says it quietly, his eyes not losing mine, a slight grin moving across his mouth, straight white teeth.

He orders a beer. I ask the waitress for a cup to take my soup out to Moonlight. "That's your dog out there, the white one? A beautiful dog." The singsong rhymey Caribbean humming in the throat.

The waitress, a very tall blonde, brings his beer and a styrofoam cup.

"I guess I'll have a beer too," I say to her, my eyes not losing his. "Your family is still in Salvador?" I ask when she's gone.

"Yes," he says. "A very pretty town. You would like it, I can tell. A pottery town on the Pacific Coast, like this. A town for artists. The tourists come there."

A wave of brutal images washes between us.

"I think of your country all the time. I'm sorry."

It's not just my country," he says, resisting, I assume, my pity. "It's happening all over the world."

The Death Squads. 17 to 35, if you're not in the army they kill you. The guerrillas turn you down, tell you to run. Not enough guns. "I've tried twice this year to go to Nicaragua, but I couldn't get the money. When were you in Salvador last?"

"Three months ago," he says, rolling his head back to drink from the bottle. He's so open.

"How did you leave?"

He shrugs, says it almost beneath his breath. "I walked."

The sun plays hypnotically on his lips, through his curly lashes.

"Sometimes I ran." A twinkle for me in his eyes. "At night, over the mountains, into Guatemala, Mexico. All the way north to El Paso. Then I swam." He grins, looking me strong in the eyes. "The Rio Grande." He says it with the Spanish e. "You are beautiful."

"So are you."

His manner is lacking entirely in self-pity. I'm thrilled by his walking knowledge of the continent.

"Can I ask you something personal?" His stare, the still black eyes.

Again, the little fear, the sun so strong on my face. "Yes."

"Are you married?"

"No." My biggest grin. "No! And you?"

"No. Once, but I'm divorced now."

"What are you doing in Oregon?"

"I'm taking a little vacation. I've never traveled in this country. In the morning I'm going to Eugene, Highway 126, then I-5 to Portland."

The images of his running the North American continent are already deep in me. *Vacation* is such a different notion. North, though. He's still going north.

"Isn't there danger in being stopped?" Immigration, it says right on this bulletin board, is cracking down, making it harder to get jobs.

"I was stopped yesterday," he says, "for speeding, coming up 101. I had to pay sixty dollars, but the DMV doesn't care about your birthplace, or ask questions." He pulls out his driver's license.

The picture is of a man with a long Afro and a thick curly moustache. It's hard to see that it's the same person. Now he's clean shaven in the style of the times with very short hair. *Francisco Allonso Modesto.* The address is Figueroa Street in Los Angeles. A flood of images from my old neighborhood. Even then, ten years ago, it was filling with Central and South American immigrants. Now 200,000 Salvadorans in LA. In San Diego, along the border, people leave food outside their doors at night for the refugees.

"How old are you?" I ask after handing back the license. I forgot to look. I feel the rush of the beer. I can't believe it, the jukebox is playing Bruce Springsteen's "Born In The U.S.A."

I hear 22. He speaks perfect English though occasionally I can't understand through the accent.

"Am I old enough? Do you want to get married?"

"Married?" I laugh. "I have to go to Minneapolis on Monday."

"Let's go together. I have a Toyota with a camper on the back. That's how I travel. That way I don't have the expense of motels."

I laugh again. All I need is another man.

"You understand," he says, leaning toward me. "I'm really on my way to Canada. To seek political asylum."

I am caught by his hands, the long slender fingers, the dark stains between each. His face. I see all the races playing in it. Indian, Spanish, African chiseled with light, Anglo, a golden smoke like sunset. His eyes are large and so dark I can't tell the pupils from the irises. They are black marbles as he answers my questions.

"I would be on the side of the guerrillas if I was there."

But he is not there and I think I see that he is not a fighter. There is too much acceptance in him to take sides to kill. Libra, I bet. Lover. An innate sweetness untouched by heinous witness. Still, his eyes do not absorb me the way the rest of his face and body and being do.

They are the one hint of violence his country is undergoing.

"Canada," he says. "Or I could marry an American girl."

"Oh." I look at him, understanding now his question. "I'm sorry. Legally, I am married. I haven't been with the man for fifteen years but I never divorced him. I could never see a reason to." I reach for his hand. "I'd marry you, today, right now, Francisco." After all these years I'm encountering a reason to be legally divorced! I could really help him, someone like him.

"You can get a divorce. We can go in the morning to Eugene, find a lawyer."

"It costs too much, takes too much time."

"No. I have the money. It'll be easy." Now he reaches across the table for my hand. A pelican, as if in response, flaps its huge awkward wings, flies off. The waitress brings two more beers.

"I'm from LA too," I say, stalling. "But it's been a long time. That's where my old husband is. What about your wife?"

"Yes, she's there" My *ex*-wife," he corrects me, letting go my hand. Emotion like a rip tide races through the skin, the first I've seen. "She fell in love with a Mexican. She's married to him now."

I watch a fishing boat coming in beneath the bridge as he tells me they first came to the United States in 1976. They were students. "First we had to learn English. We went to a special school in Los Angeles. Then we had a baby. A son." When his wife fell in love with the Mexican he moved to San Francisco, the Mission district, went to school. Worked for a long time in a restaurant on Fisherman's Wharf. A year ago he moved to Santa Cruz to study computers.

"And you were in Salvador just three months ago?"

"It's my country. I go back many times. My grandma is 93. But I can't study there. They closed the university." He sighs. "And this time someone killed my friend."

He puts his hand to his cheek, dusty and gold at the same time. Modesto. Modest. I'm taking a little vacation now. I'm moving, he puts it another way. Everything I own is in the camper. He seems to trust me. I can't get used to this. I'm paranoid for him. He's not paranoid because he's lived in very hip California towns. What will happen to him when he travels east and north where the values and politics are so different? Where there's racism. Perhaps, in his clarity, the graceful positivism he exudes, he finds the safe path, his armor. These thoughts oppose the growing ones of the brutal losses he's known, which become a fear of him. A fear I would have of anyone with such a story. I feel him in danger and dangerous at the same time.

"I want to go to Quebec where they speak French," he says. "I don't like the cold, but they might give me asylum. The U.S. won't."

"Minnesota is on the way to Quebec," I say with a sigh. More and more I can see it, our going together.

"It is?" His black eyes are like walls without doors or windows. "You can leave your car here, go in mine. You can sell it."

"I'm sorry. I've already made the commitment to go with someone else." Just go with this man, you can help him. And he can teach you about Central America. I think of how apolitical Joey is, the aspect I least respect in him. But then I think of trying to tell him, of breaking my commitment. And though I'd marry this stranger on the spot, to make the commitment to travel across the country with him is something far more serious.

It's past four already. "I have to go to the garage where my van is," I say, gathering up my things.

"We can go in my truck."

"No. I need to walk, and then I have to go home. I have so much to do I'm not going to get any sleep in the next three days."

Moonlight greets us at the door. The wind is blowing hard. I hold the cup so he can lick out the clam chowder. Francisco watches me. Does he see the homeless refugee? We walk past a group of fishermen on the dock. A new friend, Tony, is in the center of them. Our eyes meet, then his dart to Francisco, then he looks away, not acknowledging me. We get off the wharf, head up funky Bay Street.

Will you have dinner with me after you get your van? I'm not hungry and I can't take the time. I have to pack, clean my parents' house, finish a story, and cocktail two more nights at the lodge. Well, then, at least a drink? But I must already be drunk because when I turn to him I'm a little in love with him and he knows it.

He points out his blue Toyota camper parked in front of the Brass Whale. Packed to the brim. I feel our connection. Me and my brother on the road. I can't get over meeting him here, of all places, a Salvadoran in Wakonda Auga. We touch a lot as we walk past the dark moldy shops,most of them empty, bumping shoulders to knees. Hips. Hands. Fingers reaching out for the other's. Past Fisherman's Wharf with its red neon, OPEN 24 HOURS. "Just like San Francisco," Francisco says. I've come to love rainy Wakonda Auga in the time I've been here writing rent-free at my parents' while they're gone. Sometimes you realize it's still raining, raining hard, and you can't believe it. How could there be so much water in the sky? But now it's a rare clear afternoon. He tells of having his lunch out at the beach, the South Jetty, how beautiful it was. Another new acquaintance, Alex, is sitting at the sidewalk table outside the coffee shop with a beer reading *Tritessa*, by Jack Kerouac. I wave. He pretends he doesn't see me.

"Have you seen the movie *Sometimes A Great Notion*? Or read the book? It's about this town."

The bridge over the Wakonda Auga, with its gray concrete gothic turrets and high arches and spires, dwarfs Old Town, the west end being literally under it. Across the wide tidal river on the west side of the bridge are the enormous dunes the area is famous for, on the east the thick stands of fir and cedar, a few cabins visible in them. Along with the endless racket of gulls, the screaming of herons and moaning of foghorns and fishing boats is the constant sound of the cars on Highway 101 hitting the metal suspension section of the bridge, a violent dropping moan, then the high squeal of tires proceeding north and south the continent's edge.

We climb the bridge's embankment behind the Goodwill to the highway. The wind blows much harder up here, the cars scream by.

They call the folks—the fishermen, the dancers, the alchies, the hippies—who hang out on the river in Old Town, with its three bars in two blocks, its public sauna and junk-shops, Bay Streeters. This is a derogatory term. Many who live up here on the highway never descend below. Parents forbid their children to go down.

We walk north, bumping each other in the wind, Moonlight up ahead, back, sniffing along, big white tail wagging high. Francisco is very slender, in possession of his body, just a little taller than me. I love it when his hand grabs mine when we run across the blowy highway at the break in traffic, me shouting *Moonlight!* Then up the highway, north, holding hands.

"Do you have brothers and sisters?" My words into his ear, the wind making it hard to hear. My breath back from his warm neck.

We are crossing Devil's Point Road. I'm stepping up onto the wet curb, thinking the grip the sea has on this town, seeing beneath my white ragged tennie making the step all the particles that compose the black asphalt, the gray concrete.

"I have three brothers." I point to the garage up ahead. "There were four but someone killed my baby brother."

"Oh."

That sickness again for him, like a bullet to my heart. "You don't know who?"

"Someone. I told him not to go into the army. See, in Salvador, it is not illegal to refuse to go in. But they find you on the street and say you have to. I told my little brother not to. I told him it is bad to go into the army."

We get inside the garage. We lean against my van waiting for the mechanic. We lean into each other. His eyes into mine. His hands touching me. From such a far distance, over such a troubled land. Then I see the old mechanic looking at us, a friend of my father. I'm embarrassed but I can't seem to control us. This meeting is not a common one. Then I fear myself thinking this. El Salvador! The best line yet. I open the side door.

"Her name is Psyche."

He looks in with great interest. My purple bed. My pretty things. "Oh, this is nice. We should go to Minneapolis in this." His hand down my back.

The mechanic is the only one on duty, keeps having to run to the pumps every time a car comes in. He is cool, like Francisco, shows no annoyance or disturbance with us, though we are becoming more and more shameless, up against each other. He shows me the crack in her distributor cap. This is the reason she will hardly go. I can't see it for a long time. I remember Robin discovering a crack in the distributor cap of my last car, Roses, what none of the mechanics had been able to see. "It's because I'm on acid," he said. He keeps turning it in his gnarly hands to the west window. Smell of grease and gasoline. I think I see it but it's so tiny I can't imagine it stopping my Psyche. Then he has a customer and Francisco and I are kissing. His tongue in my mouth, the smell of oil and deep mechanics, the highway screaming out there, his face against mine, the black eyes so near. The surge and blaze and flood, so involuntary. Sleep with me tonight, marry me, let's go to Minneapolis together.

The mechanic returns, shows me the burnt rotor. I'm shaking from desire and embarrassment. A knee-weakening wet ache in my vagina. His black thumbnail traces the small burnt edge. He explains again that he is here by himself. I assure him again that it is okay to keep Psyche until morning. He keeps saying he can give me a ride home but as I told him when I brought her in, even before I met Francisco, I want to walk.

In the office a *Hustler*, a *Penthouse*, a *U.S. News and World Report*. The soldier on the cover looks like Francisco, green camouflage, rifle in his right hand, up to the shoulder, his set face just like Francisco's, not questioning, just there. His left hand at his ammo belt, the cuff rolled up once, the same slender dark wrists, fingers, and then what has caught me, held me, haunted me ever since the magazine came out, a gold wedding band on the left finger. Weakest, most vulnerable of fingers. It seems a confession. The husband who kills for her.

We walk back to Old Town, down to the river, the sun setting behind the dunes, the fishing boats coming in. I make it clear that I'm walking him to his pickup, then I'm going home.

"How?"

"Walk."

"I'll drive you."

"No. I don't want to ride. I need the exercise. It's not far." I lie. We turn the corner to Bay Street. I see his packed blue Toyota camper. I'm overwhelmed again by his situation.

"You must be lonely, Francisco."

His bumper sticker says I LOVE MYSELF.

I write out my address on a scrap of paper, my Washington post office box number, put it in his shiny blue shirt pocket. He stares into my face, moves closer.

"Please. Let's have dinner, a drink, something. I can't give you my address, I don't have one. You are right. I am lonely. I can't let you go."

"No, Francisco, I must go. Write to me, though. I will help you. Even marry you when I get back."

"Do you have a boyfriend at this address?"

"Well, yes." His face falls, his spirit changes. "I share it with a friend, but that's okay. He's a poet. He writes about Salvadoran refugees. He will help you too."

The juke box in the Brass Whale is crying *start me up*. The pinball machine and the drunks ring and clang. I start to leave. But I make the mistake of kissing him goodbye.

"I can't let you go. Oh please. I will feel terrible tonight. Let's get a motel room. Take me home with you please." His black eyes beg me. "I *am* lonely. I need you."

I feel like I'm letting the guerrillas down. Everything in me wants to unite with this man. But then waves of fear. He could be ruthless being so rootless. He's seen murder, his country raped. I shouldn't be alone with him until I know him better. Strangers turn me on only when they're unattainable. But we are standing on Bay Street necking, please, please, I beg you, sleep with me tonight, as if no one is here, as if it isn't Happy Hour. I can't resist him, my cunt throbs for him, this has never happened to me before. It's true, lately I've had more lovers than usual. I tell myself I'm studying sex, men. Breaking my self-destructive pattern of monogamy. Is this what happens to you when you start opening, there's no stopping? I even feel a wave of betrayal for Bill, though I've only known him for two weeks. What if he's driving by, seeing me?

So it's a relief to get inside the cab of his pickup, though there's hardly room for me. The Oregon DMV Instruction book is on the dash. A colorful conglomeration hangs from the rearview mirror, a scarf braided with little Indian pullstring cloths and beads and straw pockets and a button. MACHO IS NOT MUCHO. I touch it, laugh. He laughs and repeats the words lovingly in my ear, "macho is not mucho." And then his hands all down the front of my body, my hand, to stay upright, inadvertently, or advertently, on his thigh, his mucho. Into his eyes. We are kissing. I keep trying to come back, this is my father's town. People are driving by, staring, he's illegal, he's going to get caught.

"Please take me home with you. Please."

"No. I can't."

"Then let's get in the back, if you won't spend the night with me."

I look through the window to the bed. It feels like everything inside me is coming out for him. But a horn honks and I see that there's no way to get back there except to get out and crawl together through the back door.

"Francisco, we can't *here,* right on Bay Street. Everyone's getting off work, coming down for a drink."

"Well, then, we'll drive somewhere else."

"No." The same objection as to the divorce. It'll take too much time, I'll think too much. But then we are all over each other again, my tongue in his mouth, his hand in my wet levi crotch.

"What are you doing, Fella?"

An enormous man in his late fifties is stooped to my window, leering in. He must have seen me pulling away, resisting, this black guy molesting this blonde right here on Bay Street.

Assuming my most adult manner, I roll down the window, at the same time tell Francisco to start the engine, let's get out of here, tell the man it's okay, everything is fine, the reek of alcohol on his breath filling the little cab, his red-gray hair wild in the window about what this fellow is doing to me.

"We're fine, Mister. We're old friends, we just haven't seen each other in years." I lay my hand on his wooly plaid arm. Come on Francisco, start the engine.

But very quickly the drunk man changes. "Oh. Alright." He reaches his huge arm in across my face to shake Francisco's hand. "How ya doin, Fella?"

"Fine, man," Francisco says. "How are you doing?"

I think this redneck has looked into this Salvadoran refugee's face and seen the lover too and like me cannot resist him.

It's getting dark. The undercurve of my breasts ache to be cupped, lifted in his long hands, the nipples sucked. My whole body longs for his body on top of it. Finally I agree to have a drink with him. Something to kill the resistance.

The Bridgetown is one of those establishments you find in many coastal towns like Wakonda Auga. It's the original hotel, a hundred years old, recently renovated. The Bridgetown opened during the summer, adding a little class to seedy Bay Street. This is due to the prices and the decor. A palm tree, Hawaiian motif . . . or perhaps it's Southern California.

We sit in the darkest corner, high back, white wicker chairs. I watch the soft swish of the sexy litttle belly beneath the long Hawaiian print shirt of the gay waiter as he comes toward us. Ceremoniously, he lights our candle. I order a brandy in a heated snifter, finally giving up my evening to Francisco. Francisco orders a Grand Marnier, with a beer back.

"I saw this girl in the corner," he says, looking deep into my eyes. "Blond curls all down her red sweater. I love your hair." He touches it. "I love your hair."

Already we are drawing too close to each other, in danger again of being too public.

"Do you want to have a baby?" he asks.

"Oh, *yes*. I do." The question takes me by surprise. How long I have longed to have another baby, none of my men willing.

"I was raised on a farm by grandma. She is 93."

"What about your mother?" Smoothing down my hair where he's pulled it out.

"She died. When I was five. I had four brothers, two older than me, two younger. So her mother raised us."

The most orphan fact of all.

"How did she die?" I can hardly ask this.

"A heart attack." he says it tenderly, as of a child. "She was 36. Isn't it funny, her mother has lived so long. My mother was very beautiful."

"And your father?"

"My father was crazy after my mother died." His curly lashes flicker across my candle view of the Bridgetown. I see him running north, nights. "Somebody kept trespassing across our land. He had a garden in the back, but every night someone walked through it, stomping down his crop. He put up a fence, then he put up signs, but he was out of his mind with grief. He shot someone. So he was in prison for twenty years."

I feel my eyes taking on his stare. "You must be older than 22." It's the only thing I can think to say.

"I was born September 25, 1951." He is putting the open part of my hand to his mouth, his tongue, then turning his face in it. "Am I old enough?"

"September 25 is my son's birthday." The words like flesh caught in my throat.

"You have children?"

"They're grown."

"Did you raise them?"

"I wouldn't have let anyone else do it."

"And you want to do it again?"

"To keep them from sending you back to be killed? I'd marry you in a second, tomorrow. I would have your baby." *There are women who will do this for you, Francisco.* "But, in fact, I am married."

"Let's go to a lawyer in the morning. In Eugene."

"No. I can't now. But write to me. Maybe we can do it later." I don't know how to explain to him that it will take too much time. I *have* to leave for Minnesota. My life is far too complicated as it is to be healthy. A divorce will take months. I can't be engaged to him. I can only marry him.

"I have money. We'll just do it. Fifteen years. Isn't there a common law divorce?"

"I don't think so." How to explain to him, a Libra, my avoidance of institutions—religious, medical, educational, civil—that I'm not a legitimist.

"Are you a Catholic?" I ask. His problem is legitimacy.

"Yes!" This seems to settle him. "Yes, I am. I mean I don't go to Mass, but I'm a Catholic. Are you?"

I shake my head, sorry again to disappoint him, see myself walking down the aisle beneath a bridal veil, submitting to all of it, baptism, babies. El Salvador.

"My brother lives in Modesto, California." I love his face, the love in it. "And you don't see your son?"

"My son remembers me." He pulls out his wallet again, shows me a little boy. "This is my son, Allonso."

Allonso laughs his one year at me, his fat bare leg curled beneath his bottom.

"They say I wasn't a good father. My wife was in love with a Mexican. I threw a big party for his first birthday. For everyone to come, all our friends in Los Angeles. But my wife's mother, she didn't like it that I got drunk, she said I was carrying my son around by the neck, I was holding him like this." He crooked his arm. "I was carrying him in here, by the neck, singing and singing. My son," he adds, with rigid assurance, swallowing his Grand Marnier, "remembers me."

Again I am searching his face for hatred, bitterness, violence.

"How can one person take so much, Francisco? You've lost everything."

"I'm just glad," he says, so simply, "to be alive."

His bumper sticker. If I passed him on the freeway I'd be annoyed by the narcissism.

"How do you make sense of any of it? How did it get so bad in Salvador? And why?" I see film clips of one day in 1932. The U.S. Marines invade. 30,000 people massacred. I can't see pain in Francisco but I can see his country, the mountains and the sea and the border that is Guatemala, and Honduras, the sweep down past the Mayan pyramids to the sea. I can see the farm he grew up on, his pretty coastal town, the potters at their clay.

"What would we do if we married?"

"I have plans. It will not always be this way. I will study computers. I want a family, children. You want to have a baby?"

"Sí."

I'm sure it's important to have a Salvadoran. "Sí." But this would never work under ordinary circumstances. The husband I left fifteen years ago was in computers.

"Then let's do it. Please."

Now it seems I made a mistake. To have gone with Joey over this man. To have not gotten the divorce, married him. But I was already on the road to Minneapolis, the poetry reading there would be all the money I'd made for the rest of the year, Psyche's garage bill was being paid for by Joey, and I couldn't be sure about Francisco. Friends tell me now there are no blacks in El Salvador, suggesting all sorts of intrigue. My recent publications had been followed by a number of strange incidents that had caused me to think that my old FBI file had been re-activated. Or could my eyes have deceived me? Maybe Francisco was Indian. The urge to lay with him was so powerful as to make me afraid of him. It certainly could have altered my perception.

"I can't move this fast, Francisco. You have my address." I take it out of his shirt pocket, jot down my parents' phone number and two Washington telephone numbers. "I will help you in any way I can. I won't let them take you back to Salvador, but right now I can't go to Minneapolis with you. I apologize if I led you to believe that I would. But you can meet me there on your way to Quebec. November 18." I write the Minneapolis number.

"Can we go to your house then for the night?"

"No. It would hurt my father." It is a relief to think of this. I see that he will honor my father.

"Haven't you ever found anyone else to marry?"

He tells me about Windy, "a white girl from Pennsylvania." The same confusion, the wave of emotion, a loss of energy, across his face. He loved her. A year ago she went back to her husband. "She wanted to keep seeing us both but I said to her if you love your husband you should go back to him. That really hurt." I can see that it did. Love and war, what matters most? Loss of country, mother, father, brother, friends, none of these register in Francisco. The loss of women does. His son.

He orders another Grand Marnier, a beer back. I still have half my brandy. "I'm going to get drunk tonight and it's your fault," he says.

When the waiter returns, balancing his tray, I ask for the time.

"Ocho y diez," he says.

"Gracias," Francisco and I say in unison. It's so late.

I swallow all of my brandy. "Who was the last person you fucked?"

"You want to know?" he asks, surprised.

I feel the switch. If we are not to be married, then we will get into naughty sex.

"Yeah," giggling. "You tell me, I'll tell you." Our hands again all over each other, both of us leaning into the other's seat. My lips on his warm soft neck.

The candle flickers from a draft of the wind. The radio is saying the wind is blowing 90 miles an hour through Southern Oregon. His face is suddenly very open, very serious. He kisses me with his full lips.

"Two nights ago, in Arcata. I hadn't had a bath since I started on my vacation. So I looked in the yellow pages for a public hot tub." I love his face, the color of it. "I was having a coke before my bath and this woman came in. We talked a few minutes, she asked where I was from and then I asked her if she'd like to have a hot tub. She said sure."

It seems he is going to stop his tale there so I ask further. But all he will say is that it was wonderful. "And then she was gone. Not even an address, a phone number. When I asked her for them she said no. That's all. And she was gone. I'll never see her again."

Women helping this refuge on up the coast to the next country, to political asylum.

"And before that?"

"In Santa Cruz. I met a woman in a bar. She was young. I bought her drinks and she invited me to her place. We were beginning to make love when she said she needed the money now. What do you mean? I mean I'm a working girl. She was a prostitute. What could I do? I was already undressed. And before that, it was a long time, a year. Last August. With Windy, when she decided to go back to her husband."

"The girl in the hot tub?"

"Yes?"

"What did you feel about her? I mean in terms of Catholicism, you know, the double standard. Machismo. The Latin male."

"I loved her for letting me do with her as I wanted. I don't feel those things, that she was immoral, or cheap. No, I loved her."

He pulls from his drink. "You mean like some men have a wife and a mistress?"

"Well, yes," remembering the interview of the Sandinistas in *Playboy* a few months ago, how much it exposed their sexism, their Old World Patriarchism. I think of the women guerrillas who like

Francisco have lost everything, plus one other loss, maybe the worst of all, faith in men. In battle, in hell, they've been made to know sexism.

"Some men do it. They have a wife and they have mistresses. It is just what they do. But not all men. I don't. I don't agree with that way."

I believe him, though I can hear my non-Latin-mechanic-on-acid's answer to the same inquiry. "You look right in your woman's eyes and you lie." Francisco's life was so blown apart I have to believe this. Then I think how all the refugees seem to be men. Is Salvador a country now of just women, children and the Death Squads?

My elbows hurt from leaning into his wicker chair. I worry again that our amorous behaviour is calling attention to him, endangering him, but no one, the bartender, the waiters, or customers, seems askance. At the center of so much violence, Francisco himself seems not to attract violence. I don't understand the karma in this but it must be how he survives.

The waiter brings another round.

"Okay," he says, "Your turn to tell me."

I think on it a minute, fearing betrayal of someone I love.

"A man from New Zealand. I met him in the Brass Whale two weeks ago. He's a monogamist."

"A monogamist?"

"Yes! That's how he introduced himself to me! His wife is a feminist, he said, who believes in fucking many men. He couldn't take it. He tried, for two years, but finally he left, left the country."

"When?"

"Sunday night. Two nights ago, the last time. Must have been the same as you. He was very good for me. Interesting. I'd never experienced the monogamist spirit in a man before."

"What do you mean?"

"I could feel it, powerful, surging all through him. It was running the whole length of his body. It was incredibly sexy. He said he was part Maori, that it's his strength."

"Do you like to fuck?"

"How do you say I want to fuck you in Spanish?"

"Yo voy a cojere contigo."

"You voy a cojere contigo, Francisco Allonso Modesto. Sí?"

"Sí."

We lean back in our white wicker chairs, grinning. I can see him in Quebec, wandering the old frozen streets, so European.

"Can we go to your house?"

I see us in my parents' bathtub, all the mirrors. I see him bathing me. "Would you promise to leave in the morning?"

He promises. He stares ahead in thought. "I want to have a family, money, things. I want children. I don't like this life, of one night stands."

"Would you take me to Salvador?"

His response is great. "You want to go?"

"Sí."

"I want to study medicine," he says excitedly. "I just want to help my people. Everyone. We could study medicine. It is the only way to go back. You want to?"

Then he mentions a woman friend who was killed by someone. I see the photo in *Mother Jones*, a woman's decapitated head, a penis stuffed in her mouth.

"Let's go to the ocean," I say, getting up.

Moonlight greets us at the door, jumping both paws to my breasts. Then he charges to Francisco's truck, somehow knowing. We get out into the wind. Francisco moves toward a shadow to piss. I follow him, fold into his back away from the fury and the spray, my arms around his waist. I keep trying to think about taking him to my parents' house.

We drive out Devil's Point Road, the pickup rocking in the rain and wind. This man could be a killer. Maggie goes to Salvador, her stories, how they've gone stark raving mad. They *like* to kill now. Once you start killing you get into it. It's addictive. I don't feel any of this in him. It's mysterious how I can detect no violence in him, not even what's in myself.

We sweep right by the drive.

"I want to walk into the Pacific with you, Francisco. The Pacific Ocean! The same water that laps El Salvador!"

The sea is wild. It always is here, even when the weather is mild, even now at low tide. The rock walls stretches to an inch beneath the black horizon, North Jetty I last walked with my Uncle C.D. just before he died. "If I was young I'd live like you," he said at the end. We were almost swept off.

We walk a long way trying to reach the water, the wind crazing and whipping, Moonlight leaping and barking. Francisco's reluctant so I pull him along. "I want to go into the sea with you, then everything we do will be holy." The sea keeps receding. It is very dark, the stars blowing out of their constellations, the moon between new and the first quarter, gone already in Capricorn. When the moon is in Capricorn I don't make mistakes. But the sea keeps leaving, the wind whips at us with sand and flying kelp like a sadist, blowing in what will be reported as the strongest wind of the decade. El Niño. Its roar makes it impossible to talk. My leather jacket feels like it's being shredded. I pull it off, then my shoes, levis, sweater, underwear, stuff everything beneath a giant driftwood tree. He looks at me apprehensively. "Take your clothes off!" But he doesn't. We keep pushing to reach it, phosphorous igniting in its long churning ribbons, until finally a clear flow of water sweeps to us. We stop, cling to each other. It washes around our ankles. I run into the next wave with Moonlight, dipping and splashing the water everywhere, my face, my breasts. A wave splashes into my crotch. Moonlight barks at the wave, at my crotch. Then we are running backwards, laughing, trying to beat the next one, then turning, sweeping up my clothes, runnning all the way back through the sand and wind to the truck.

Again, we embrace. "I have to pee," he says, pulling away. I follow him, pulling on my sweater, my jacket, loving the gritty sand on my skin, feeling already the inner warmth that comes from a cold dip. "Can I stay with you, you don't mind do you? Oh, I love you, I love the world!" I shout it to the Milky Way. "I'll drink your piss!" leaning into his back again, holding onto his narrow waist.

"You will? You want to?"

"Well, yeah." A little surprised. "I guess. Do you do that in your country?"

"I've never done it, you want to?"

"Sure. I'll try anyway."

The wind is roaring 90 miles an hour through Oregon, I'm giggling, sure, I'd love to do something to commemorate this special meeting, I've always wondered what urine tastes like. I look into his face first.

"Is it okay, Francisco?"

"I love you," he says.

So I trust him. Laughing, I kneel to his crotch, put my mouth over his penis. O most familiar, fantastic form! His macho is the size of most men's and as awesomely delicate as all. He's saying above me in the wind I don't know if I *can* piss in your mouth and I'm not sure I can take it, a gust of fear with the screech of a gull, I just wait, I can feel him concentrating, holding my mouth over him, about half way up, waiting in the slamming wind, this is different than sucking him off, this is urine, you just wait, my bare knees hurting in the sand and gravel, but I'm so glad he's so willing, what a Venus man, what a lover, so sweet, so willing to do anything, oh, I will drink his urine, I love him I love us I love the world! Then I can feel all the machinations of the body, I'm inside him, at one with him, this isn't ejaculation, this is another function, like my own, like everyone who lives, my sisters how many times a day, this is the body, all of humanity, this is the river into the sea, this is the same water from the beginning of time, this is the mind in the bladder, the urethra, the blessed penis, and then after what seems a very long and willful time, I feel the release, I know the urine beginning its journey, I know it's coming, and then it pours gently into my mouth.

Water! As if from a drinking fountain, a water hose. It's water! O

Ken Kesey, O Wakonda Auga forever, El Niño, Anna Livia Plurabella to the river Liffey, it's *water!*

One swallow, two. Enough. Letting go, pulling back, gulping again, laughing as I rise, water! It's water, Francisco! He turns in the other direction, his laughter carrying past me like a gull on the wind. No, he laughs, it's beer.

We drive back, speeding down Devil's Point Road, Moonlight wet and smelly between us. I've decided to take him to the house, to just relax, not worry, to sleep with him, make warm love in all the shiny mirrors, let him have a good night's sleep in my parents' kingsize. But then I'm seeing again how impossible it is for me to say no to him, to anything he wants. I would marry him on the spot. There's no question about being a nurse in Salvador. Meet his grandma and live in his artist town and be a guerrilla and drink his piss and have his babies. I keep practicing the words, it's up here, around this corner, the next drive to the right. Forgive me, Daddy. But the curve surprises me, we're on it so quick, my throat closes down to dumbness. Waves of nostalgia, regret, loneliness and relief pass through me as we sweep by my driveway. Forgive me, Francisco. Better to fuck in the back.

"Where shall we go?" he asks.

"Some place to sleep."

"I always sleep in motel parking lots."

"The owners don't bother you? I usually sleep in rest stops but there aren't any near here."

"No, the best places are motel parking lots."

"Okay, then go south up here." Then I remember. "Do you have contraceptives?"

"No."

"Well, then, go north. We have to get some. I'll get pregnant."

I point the way to Safeway. I wait as he goes in, Moonlight between my legs, the Eagle's tape "Hotel California" playing. I'm very warm now from going in the ocean, my skin tingles from the salt. I watch him move around inside the flourescent cavern that is Safeway. A small dark man. I think of that girl in the hot tub two nights ago. This must be how diseases spread because I'm committed. I'm going to fuck him. Rubbers will help. I watch him go to the aisle, disappear down it, then come back, empty-handed, this could be heaven or this could be hell, he is whispering in the ear of the teenage boy cashier, the cashier is telling him something complicated, pointing and gesturing with his hands, and then Francisco is coming through the automatic doors, this Salvadoran wetback, did you see the movie *Border*? I asked him in the hotel, he grinned yes and I see dark figures stooped with packs walking the train tracks north through Ashland in the middle of last winter, I think of Patrick and Bill and Joey, I want to love this man no matter what, but he's coming through the automatic doors and now into the truck empty-handed.

"They don't have condoms here," he says, sinking into the driver's seat. "He said the only place you can get them now is in the men's bathroom at Fisherman's Wharf."

I think fast. Diaphragm's in my bag, I *must* have $5.00, I hate to spend it since there's a tube at home, but the way I'm studying sex these days I'll need it soon enough anyway. I jump out of the truck, descend into the fluorescence, buy the stuff, Ramses, not Gynol, horrible yeast infections, the years I put stickers announcing this on every contraceptive rack I encountered, look the boy in the eyes, he doesn't flinch, blink, grin, flirt, or otherwise acknowledge my purchase. Safeway's rather than the Wharf's. Until as I grab the sack he's thrown it in and turn out of his aisle and move toward the doors, Francisco watching me, I see in the window's reflection the jerk of the boy's head to the other boy sweeping the floor, I remember a party last summer in Port Townsend, the only folks I know there with a hot tub and we are all cool but later there is a woman outside or a couple because a fully-dressed young man is a little out of his mind and body or too deep in them, that strange sex fix, close to drooling, as he stares from the dark bedroom into the black glass of the patio.

Back down the highway, south, the wind making it hard to steer. Across the turreted bridge, the slip, whine of our tires when we hit the metal center that opens to the tall ships. The Wakonda Auga down there. The wind screaming Kesey's "Goodnight Irene." The motel on the east side. Turn here. Instantly we are enshrouded in tall firs, darkness and stillness, a descent half-way down to the river. He pulls into the furthest parking place, away from the long building, the two other cars.

Then I'm afraid. I'm always afraid at this moment. I am so inadequate.

We get out to pee, the three of us. I started hoarding tissue in my pockets in the hotel. Moonlight and I go down the river road. It's beginning to sprinkle. Wonder if I'm okay. Where I am. I feel the little tear before this act, the great monogamist spirit within me who has so often broken my heart. Wishing it was Patrick. Only an occasional starlight flash of the river but its nearness, its passing dominates, or rather saturates everything. Pissing into the little stream of water flowing down the asphalt road to the Wakonda Auga, two miles then to the Pacific. The wind rushes through my thighs in that old childhood tune from Tijuana radio, *the sea will grow large with my tears.*

He is standing at the back door of the camper with his shirt off, in longjohns.

I crawl headfirst into the tiny compartment. It is crammed with his things, just a lying-down space, a fucking space if she won't take you to her father's bed. The overhead light is so close, a foot or two above me. I pull off my clothes. He crawls in, having taken off his pants outside. He starts unbuttoning his longjohns and I sit up, as well as I can, find my diaphragm, squeeze out the jelly. Rolling back, legs raised, inserting it. Once I could not have done this in his presence. Then he is over me, his smooth smokey skin and insistent tongue, his hands down my breasts, inserting his unquestionably black genital into mine.

How wonderful it feels, as always. He plays, a little too manic, with my left nipple. As always, I am too manic. I succumb and enjoy our mania.

We move in and out of each other for a long time, sometimes very tenderly, my vagina milking his cock, sometimes pounding with lust, his cock drilling my cunt, watching each other, all the images, all the places, the rain beginning, beating at the camper top. His hand on my face, his finger, two fingers, three in my mouth. We beat at each other until sweat is running off both our bodies, till we are slipping and sliding in our water. Inside and outside. After a while I realize he is waiting for me to come. I had forgotten about this, I'm in a kind of trance, of the moment, without goal or destiny. He pulls out of me then. I turn over to climb on top but am stopped by the iridescent color of his skin, so beautiful, gun metal. And then a long scar, and bullet holes.

The scar is surgical, slices his trunk exactly in two, from beneath his nipples to below the delicate round of his gray belly, the pubic line. Hard knots, I know are bullet scars though I've never seen any, are scattered everywhere. He has no navel. It is sewed up.

"What is this from, Francisco?"

"They had to cut me open. I would have died."

"And these?"

"Bullets."

"But who?" Running my hands down the scar, and again, and again, kissing the knots, from his tight hairless chest all the way down to his deep black penis. How dark his penis is, so much darker than the rest of him. Oh, I love you Francisco. I put it in my mouth, make it large again.

"My brother and I were walking down the street in our town when they came, said we had to go into the army. I told my brother to refuse to go. They took us to a room." I'm looking into his calm, unemotional face. "I saw him fall."

Now to touch him, the hard little knots beneath his heart, oh to love him to fuck him, el niño, that someone would kill you, I am crying. He asks me how do I make you come? Sometimes I come this way, weeping and weeping, surprise, an orgasm out of tears, and maybe another, now bawling. But not this time. I don't want to. I can't aggress upon him, use him for myself. I am too moved, paralyzed in my witness of him, of all the evil aggression put upon him. The muscle in my vagina pumps and pulls him in an involuntary spasm I've only known from multiple orgasms but I don't come. I turn over and he puts it in from behind. He rises off me, crying out.

When he falls back to me we lie very quiet, the cloth on which my face lies soaking with tears. They are streaming out, though now sound isn't. After a while he rolls off, turns out the light, sleeps.

Now I feel the brandy. I feel much deeper my whole year, homeless. I am so tired. I touch my own scar. The rain and wind blows against the little truck, the trees swish and scrape against themselves. I wonder where Moonlight is taking shelter. Far off, above us, an occasional car sweeps up or down the coast, the plunk and high whine and rolling of the tires in the song that is Wakonda Auga. We fit in here as in a cocoon. Our wedding night.

I never forget where I am. In a sort of trance, not peaceful, more like prayer, awaiting instructions. As I could find no desire to come I find none to sleep or to leave. I smell dirty socks. I pull out the bunched cloth beneath me. His longjohns. Again I'm awed by his easiness about everything. I love him for this. I love him for how Northamerican he has become, his profound adaptation. I love lying beside him sleeping, his semen trickling out now, down the fat of my buttocks. Feeling for the tissue I hid when I crawled in. Try to think about leaving. Drift off in the trance, two more nights of cocktailing, then the trip with Joey to Minneapolis, will I see Bill again? the warmth and intimacy of this bed, feeling privileged to be in here, to share of him this way, not wanting ever to leave this moment, then coming to, where I am, the rain and wind hitting us, a little amazed that I really am going to leave, walk all the way home in the middle of the night in the driving rain. When I doze off, the images of the night, his grandma, his running the mountains and swimming the rivers, north and north, all the men running from that country come at me like the rain and out of me like semen.

I don't move until I can wait no longer. Have to pee. I locate my levis stuffed around my feet and the back door. I hope I can dress and get out without waking him. I pull on my pants, wiping away the stuff again.

"What are you doing?"

"I have to go home, Francisco."

"I'll drive you."

"No. I really do want to walk."

"It's raining. Hard."

"I'll love it."

I find my backpack, my jacket, kiss him goodbye.

"Francisco, you must promise you'll write to me."

"Okay."

I know he won't.

"Please know this, Francisco, if you get in trouble, call those numbers. I will not let them take you back." We have been into so many wild fantasies with each other how can he believe me? "I know a few people."

I move my hand down his smokey body, the black bullet holes, tears welling again. I drank his piss so he'd believe me.

"I love you, Francisco."

"I love you too." He catches the water on his tongue. "Will you be okay?"

"Oh yes! I'll love walking in the storm."

We kiss again. My hand on his face. Scoot out the back door, slam it shut.

The rain hits me like a hose. The wind tears open my sweater. I hurry to put on the jacket Joey gave me, zip it up, button the fur collar around my neck. My hair flies everywhere. Semen spills out. Moonlight leaps for joy to see me. I feel a little dizzy, spaced. Walk down the road again to pee, squatting over the river beside the blackberry bushes, wet thorns and leaves and rain on my ass, find a fat juicy blackberry, so sweet, his pee from inside me. Moonlight smelling us. When I come back up past the truck, I blow him a kiss asleep inside, climb the hill, through the parking lot and out to the highway. North.

The night is water, the rain pouring through it like a river. Fear shoots through me. Fear of the bridge. To walk across it in the dark, in the rain and wind. I'm approaching it for a half mile, ducking into the bushes when a car comes, headlights blinding me. The bridge seems to sway though it's concrete, the rain like intention, the river menacing, churning beneath me through the dunes. I chant "The Bridge," *and we have seen night lifted in thine arms.* I feel sad and happy at the same time. Exhilarated by my circumstances, deeply saddened by them. I'm a refugee running north. I'm a wetback swimming the border. I'm not alone, I have my dog, *Albion Moonlight*! As I hit the metal I dread a car coming. No bushes to hide in. I almost pray. *Hands of the curveship lend a myth to God.* I choose the west side of the bridge, the ocean side, against the traffic. Is there a walk for pedestrians? Down in Old Town I've wondered this so often. Can I walk across the bridge? I trip over something, clang of metal, Moonlight, this side, that, his body electric white. The rabbit foot on my zipper bounces beneath my throat. Halfway across Moonlight disappears. I call him, walk back, search. He's nowhere. The bridge is so long, so high, so complicated in its arches and spires and turrets, its metal floor, its many sections. Could he have blown off? Fallen into the center where it opens for ships? Gone back to Francisco? Moonlight's the one I can't lose, the loss I won't be able to take. Two or three minutes of hysteria, grief, searching, calling, then he comes from the direction we came, through the pouring rain, white streak sniffing the metal road, this side, that, exhilarated too. Now I'm afraid he'll get hit by a car, or cause a car to wreck, drive off. I'm afraid to run, afraid of tripping over the metal suspension parts, I feel someone looking at me from the dark water, someone like all of Francisco's someones, then I think pelicans, its just the pelicans, and the whales, *Only in darkness is thy shadow clear*, I see the pod of whales that beached here a few winters ago and died, I walk as fast as I can to beat any car coming in either direction, slow enough to be cautious, the dread of being trapped in their headlights with no place to hide making my heart race. Now a car coming from behind, guys leaving the lodge. I hit the grooved suspension again, the whispery pattering of my rubbery soles. Now I can see Old Town beyond the third turret, beneath the arch, way down on the river. Fisherman's Wharf, the only condoms in town, blinking the rain with red neon OPEN 24 HOURS. The people sitting in there just like Kesey's folks twenty years ago. I'm soaked, my crotch soaked all the way through with semen, the wind hitting it, the river's cold moving up and into me, deep shivers. My life on the run. Me and my jacket, my white tennies, their ragged holes, the beaded frendship pen Chava pinned to my laces last summer in Port Townsend, this town I've had three lovers in. The grand grace of Bill that night we danced at the lodge so like the monogamous couple, my parents' town. My beautiful parents. And still, even still, I am their naughty daughter. This makes me laugh, skip, run through the pouring driving surging crazed El Niño so many hundreds of feet over the river draining Oregon already awash in the sea pouring into it, in and out every six hours of eternity, the dunes like enormous Moby Dicks beneath the stars. Giant face of the bull looking straight down on me.

The car still coming. *Moonlight*! Now it hits the metal center, wham, whang, and moan the town's chorus, I'm running, just your neighborhood jogger, my obedient watchdog at my heels. The truck passes, is off the bridge, the driver looks back, is way up ahead slowing down before I realize, *Francisco*. He pulls across the highway into the Ragan Motel and waits beneath the peeling unlit sign.

I'm approaching a long time though I'm running, my hands shoved deep in my pockets, my hair wet, electric wires in the wind. His am radio from Santa Rosa singing the rain down in Africa, his bumpersticker luminescent in the dark. I LOVE MYSELF. I feel in my pocket a tube of lipstick, *Luminescent Violet.* I put it on at a trot, howling at myself.

"See, Francisco!" Touching his shiny blue shoulder through the window. "There's no such thing as divorce."

NO MAN'S LAND

When I was a girl, I knew I was a man
because they might send me to Alcatraz
and only men went to Alcatraz.
Sharon Olds

Goddamn it, Jimmy. You motherfucker. Come out of there.

(A woman's voice)

◇ ◇ ◇

Jimmy just come down far enough to talk to me, no one wants to hurt you.

Jimmy I don't want to get your mother involved. If we have to I'll bring her down.

Jimmy this is your Uncle Bob. You gotta come outta there. Give me some kind of sign, Jimmy, some kind of sign. We know you're in there. No body wants to hurt you.

Goddamn it Jimmy. You're gonna come out here and talk.

(A man's voice)

◇ ◇ ◇

Starr and I are crouched on the floor of her writing porch on the dark second floor of 3020 Southeast Yamhill, in Portland, Oregon. She's moved out the typewriter and chair to make room for us.

"What's the moon in?" I whisper, thinking *Gemini, the sun's in*

Gemini.

"Scorpio," she hisses.

Our eyes lock. *"Fuck!"*

◇ ◇ ◇

We'd met in front of the downtown library. Friday night energy surged through the city like one of its great rivers. She was sitting on the steps reading a book wearing an Albert Einstein mask beneath a black fedora hat. A Sherlock Holmes black-and-white checkered raincoat. I sat down at the feet. Einstein looked up from the book, *Writing Like A Woman.*

"You recognized me."

"It's your new shoes," I said, patting the weaved top of the left one which bobbed over her right calf.

"Can you tell they're men's? I have a hard time, tens-and-a-halves. I go all over the city. These were in the window. I ran in, exclaiming 'You have human size shoes!' 'No,' the clerk said, 'Those are men's'"

I get lost in Portland, so I followed her east across the Willamette River to Southeast Yamhill Street. Joni Mitchell sang a medley of jazz tunes, about his kids, her kid a stranger to her, and then, just as we hit the river, broke into "Unchained Melody." *Time goes by so slowly and time can do so much.* I haven't seen that movie since I was a kid but I always see the Birdman looking through the tiny crack of his Alcatraz cell across the water to San Francisco, the birds so free. I parked Psyche in the empty spot one house down from her's. "Did you know there's a Blue Moon this month?" she shouted back to me as she climbed the steps of her dilapidated Victorian. Across the street three punks were gathered on the curb. Bleached electric hair, black roots, ragged leather and denim jackets. They stared while I paralleled. I didn't look again—too electric—but a wave of immense love jolted through me. I was so glad to see them there, glad they were looking at me. I grabbed *my* leather jacket. On the stoop I was stopped by a long-haired cat—fluff-white with gold and brown streaks that ran the length of its fat body. I recognized the face, like my own face staring at me, the eyes drawn in the wide white expanse as with dark eyeliner; red heartshape lips. I'm allergic to cats but I stroked this one, jabbered at it some. I felt the ground move under my feet. *Frequent earthquakes continued to rock Mount St. Helens Friday,* the paper will put it. *The possibility of small to moderate explosive eruptions cannot be ruled out.* Starr came down the stairs wearing a Mona Lisa mask. She handed me a book of poems, *The Mother/Child Papers,* by the same author as *Writing Like A Woman.* As we pulled away—she had jammed into the tiny driveway so there was much gunning, twisting, lurching—my eyes met the cat's. A sign in the window of the large red house to the right of the punks who were also still staring at us said URBAN INDIAN COUNCIL. The paper will say the siege began at 7:30. It was past 7:30 when we pulled out of there.

We had dinner at Mars, a Chinese cafe on Hawthorne. "It's Walt Whitman's birthday," she said as we ordered.

We shared the latest about our newly adult kids. I could feel her ache for her son, like mine for my son, our boys seeming to have the hardest times out in the world. *In The Belly Of The Shark* lay beside her plate. "It's by that guy Norman Mailer got out of prison," she explained, "who then killed someone within two weeks. He admits he's not a normal person. 'How could I be?' he says, 'I've spent my whole life in prison.' In the beginning he did something minor, but 'Once they got their hands on me . . . .'"

I was glad to be with a woman, and a poet. I hadn't realized how lonely I was for this kind of thing, still in shock with my new life. I told her a little of it, of Hunter, my bronze sculptor, how we met. "I'd never experienced love at first sight, Starr. I mean that was mutual." I lifted the noodles with my chopsticks. "We agreed right off to be monogamous. I left my diaphragm under his pillow when I left for Wyoming."

She laughed with me. But then sneered, "Love is an illness."

"He wants to get married, Starr!" I was giggling now. "I've been against marriage and divorce—the law!—since I left the kid's father in my early twenties. He too! But now he says I have to get a divorce, that I'm using this philosophy as an excuse to protect myself. Oh . . . ." the words gushed past her cynicism, "in love how strange the world is, its violences. Love feels like the easiest, most natural thing."

"I've known Hunter for twenty years, did you know that?" She stared at me. Then sighed, "So tell me about Scorpio's Wrecking Yard. I've certainly heard about it."

A feeling of fierce protectiveness for Hunter swept through me. Sure he's had lots of women, but I'm the first he's wanted to marry.

"Well, we live in his old bus right in the yard with all the dead trucks. It's kind of wonderful. The bed is in the back, a loft he built with large skylights made out of jet radar caps. I'm getting to know the northern constellations. *Bootes*. I write in an old trailer parked up against his foundry. It used to store cement, so all my books and papers are getting dusted with cement."

As we talked, I felt again my enormous fear of imposing on him, the solitary life he's created in Scorpio's. "As far from the art scene as I could get," he says with scorn. But he begged me to move in. "Oh, it's a scene, Starr. Up against the railroad tracks, right under the main East-West power lines, right over the hill from the Tri-Counties Gun Club. The sound of shooting is constant. Even in the rain. The trucks too, there are major gravel pits up and down the road. I thought for a long time it was earthquakes I was waking to. Turned out to be morning dynamiting!" I laughed some more at my circumstances, seeing the truckers and Oregon farmers in Burns Brothers' Truck Plaza where I go in the afternoons sometimes to write. Depth of character like lava from their faces. Faces like Hunter's, an Eastern Oregon boy. "Scorpio's used to be a pig farm. There's a pig foetus in the freezer."

"Pigs were sacred to Demeter," she mused. A guy sat down in the booth behind her, a tiny gold loop in his left ear. Our eyes met.

“Pigs, like Pygmalion,” I punned, repressing the knife of fear. That the god of sculpture hates women.

“When it rains, Scorpio’s smells like pig urine,” I laughed. “He didn’t tell me he lived in such a place. First time I drove in, past all those dead Dodge vans, I had to talk to Psyche, it’s okay, honey, I won’t desert you. We made love for four days, then I tried to start her. She’d had a nervous breakdown! I drove halfway to Wyoming in second gear before I figured it out.”

“Your life’s like a Bruce Springsteen song,” she said.

“Bruce and Julianne got married two weeks ago just down the road! I’ve copied the photo as an announcement of my new address.”

The message in my cookie was *Forget the entanglement of love; forget not to practice charity*. I couldn’t possibly forget either at this point. I am so in love I’m having a hard time being away from him. As I was leaving he said he might go out a while. “Get out from bronze dust.” I wanted to call off my date with Starr. Something deceptive in his tone. But I couldn’t even ask him where he was going for fear I’d sound possessive. Starr’s plan was for a literary evening. We’d share new poems. But my plan was to get her to go dancing with me. I miss dancing even more than poets. Hunter keeps saying I should go dancing by myself if I want to dance, he doesn’t dance. I figured Starr would know the good places.

But when we pulled back up to her block the police had it cordoned off. Cops were everywhere, red and blue lights whirling atop their white cars. And sirens. People were running, gathering, the cars pulling over, screeching to a halt. Three cops in combat gear were leaning up against the right side of my van, with shotguns over her roof pointed to the house directly across from Starr’s. 3021.

“No, it’s not the Indians,” a guy on the corner said. “It’s the house next door.”

The punks.

“Police have a warrant out for this guy and he won’t come out. They say he’s got a gun.” The guy saying this was in shorts and sandals. “They’re taking the classic stance—shooting positions behind parked cars on Belmont too. They've called out SERT—*Special Emergency Reaction Team."* He turned and walked away, south down 30th. "Guy doesn't have a chance."

Starr came running back from talking to the cop at the cord.

"He says your van's in there until this is over! He says we can't go in!"

More police arrived.

"We could drive out to the country, go see Dane." Dane is Starr's husband.

"No!" I gasped. "I just came in from the country."

"It's 10:20. Too late for a movie."

"God, I don't want to see a movie."

"You want to hear some jazz?"

I was about to tell her I want to dance when five black ten year olds came traipsing between us, asking what's going on, man?

Starr told them.

"FU-UCK THAT!" A great girl said in the infinite authority of experience. The five never missed a step in their march south.

Starr took off again to the cops at the orange cord. I moved into the street to get a better look at the three guys on my Psyche. Hard to believe my eyes. 10:20 but it's still not dark, this is the great Northwest. A furious sky hurled indigo, streaks like fur across a cat's face, lassoing the meaty trees.

Then Starr returned, something fundamentally altered in her.

"I want to go home," she declared. Meaning her writing studio. Meaning 3020 SE Yamhill.

She led the way, down the block and around the back of the row of houses, through thick, uncut grass. Over a fence, over wet blackberry bushes. "Watch out for this wire." We dashed in the door facing Yamhill. I cringed for the bullets. Dead before we hit the door.

◇ ◇ ◇

Jimmy this is your Uncle Bob. I'm out front. Jimmy everyone figures you're armed. So there's not gonna be any games if they have to go in. Come on out.

Or gimme a sign. Lights on and off, something.

Jimmy if you'll talk flash your lights do something.

Come on Jimmy Lee gimme some kind of signal. Talk to me, man.

Jimmy.

They're gonna call you on the telephone. Just pick it up. Then go ahead and hang up. I'll call you back. All you gotta do is pick up the phone and hang it back up. And I'll know you want to talk to me.

Cause if you don't come out they're gonna come in.

The phone ringing and ringing and ringing inside the house.

Now look Jimmy . . . . .

◇ ◇ ◇

3021. The small neat house is lit up. A child's drawing of a yellow house. The front door stands open. A large hanging fern in the living room. The only light in the house itself is in the kitchen. Something orange on the refrigerator door. Starr says it's somebody sitting there but I don't think so. The house has a peaked roof. A tiny window in the peak. A large window on the right of the door, the bedroom next to the living room. The lawn is well cared for. Lavender roses, blooming purple and red rhododendrons.

The gold cat with my face is entering the front door. Her shadow, in the blazing lights, follows her in.

"The house to the left," Starr whispers behind me in the dark, "is empty." It's built on the same plan as 3021, but the grass needs mowing, there's a *For Sale* sign, and uncut roses spray in every direction. The house on the right is the Indian Urban Council. Belmont, the business street for what was once Sunnyside, the first town east of Portland, is behind the house, the rear of the Portland Credit Union sharing the alley with the rear of Jimmy's house. On the corner to our left, the second house down from the one under siege, is a house occupied by a Vietnamese family. "They must really be freaked," Starr says, *"Deja vu·"* The entire street is lined in junk cars. A small rusty sports car, yellow, with a crushed right fender, sits directly in front of the open door. A 1955 yellow and green hardtop Buick is parked nose to nose to it, silver electrical tape running down half the driver's window. I know the year and make of this car because of the poet Nick Muska: cruising around Toledo Ohio last spring in his custom 55 Buick, along the river Maumee. Directly below, on my dark left, the three armed men are still leaning their guns against Psyche. I just know they're pissing on her. I keep seeing her with bullet holes. I keep seeing the two bags of poetry I left on her bed. My van has been my home for most of the past five years, but she is almost more important to me as a symbol than as a bed on wheels. Psyche is the human soul in search of Eros.

"I think they got away," I say to Starr. "Do you know if there's a basement?"

"I should tell you," she answers. "I'm *always* on the side of the guy against the police."

"Oh yeah! No matter what. But I sure hope he comes out. They're gonna kill him, Starr."

"Jimmy you stupid son-of-a-gun.

"I wouldn't come out," I hiss loudly to the street. "If you talked to *me* that way."

You want me to bring down your mother or what?

"Yeah!" Starr and I chorus together. "Bring down his mother! She'll know how to talk to him."

I dial Hunter but get no answer. He said he might go out. In the four months I've known him he's never gone out. I've hooked myself up to a real recluse, I told Starr in Mars.

On the corner, 30th and Yamhill, behind the orange cord, the neighbors—kids, teenagers, old folks—come and go. Bicycles. Cars slowing down to take a look. The guys on Psyche are using walky talkies now. When I stick my head out the window I catch some of it. *"Around back . . . . get the light . . . Joe? Are you there?"* Starr pours cognac purchased for our literary evening. It seems a waste, really, I'm so high on this event.

"Come out Jimmy," Starr begs the house. "They're going to kill you."

There's barely room for the two of us. We take turns peering down over the sill to the green Dodge van pulled diagonally under us, from which, apparently, Uncle Bob is trying to make contact with Jimmy.

"I'm also an ambulance chaser," Starr confesses. "My Uranus in the Tenth."

"Goddess! My parents told me people like you are immoral!" We laugh, bump into each other, drink our cognac. Actually I'm the one hogging the front position. The black silhouette of a stooped cop with gun moves down the roof of the Credit Union behind Jimmy's. More cop silhouettes scurry back and forth in the alley behind the house.

"Should we leave?" she asks now from the other room. She's looking for her ghetto blaster to record Uncle Bob.

"Oh, no. I feel a sort of responsibility to Jimmy now, don't you?"

"Oh," she says. "I wouldn't go so far as to say that."

"Well. Uranus in my Sixth, on my Seventh House cusp. *Forget not to practice charity.* There must be some way, witches like us, to send him help. Bombard the house with wicca."

Jim. They're gonna blow you to Kingdom Come if you don't God damn it come out.

"Where's your paper?" I finally ask, having resisted this, my notebook in the van. "Notes For The Inquest." It's been just two weeks since an inquest jury found two Portland policemen guilty of homicide in the death of Lloyd Stevenson, a black security guard for a Northeast 7-11 Store. They killed him with a carotid artery hold, the "sleeper hold." The public inquest went on for days, the charge of racism and excessive use of force being the main issues, days of witnesses testifying, their radio voices through the wrecking yard trying to reconstruct the events, what really happened. It was my first experience with Portland as a community. They found the two police officers guilty of "criminal negligence." Though last week the Grand Jury found them innocent. And the same week, in Philadelphia, the police firebombed an entire black neighborhood for the occupants of one house, a group called MOVE. 300 people left homeless. 11 people were killed.

Time goes by so slowly and time can do so much. The house is gold now in their bluewhite lights. All our eyes on it, a meditation we're all doing together. Funny the love I felt for those punks. Wonder which one Jimmy was. A small glow deep inside the Vietnamese house, a candle. "There's an old woman in there," Starr whispers. "She's very feeble. She takes walks around the block. It takes her a long time. I think she is pondering that she finds herself in Portland in her old age."

The cat comes out the front door. A dark elongated triangle out from under her, leading off to the right. Casually she looks back over her shoulder to inside the house. The only sign the entire, long night that Jimmy, someone, is really in there.

"She's one of those bad karma cats," Starr says. "You know the kind I mean? Where you have to move across the country to get away from it and still it finds you?" I can see its glass eyes from here. "No. I don't know what her name is."

"Did you know more dry cat food is sold in Oregon than in any other state?"

"Independent cats," Starr sighs.

"My mother's father killed a man, Starr." I feel myself grinding deeper into the meditation. "In a poker game. He escaped jail with a key slipped to him in a baked potato. When they caught him, brought him back for trial he was found innocent. He'd shot in self-defense."

I notice that Starr is recording me.

"All my life I've dreamed I've committed a terrible crime, that I had no choice. And now I'm running, they're after me."

Bad Karma drops into the roses on the right of the porch. A girl in tight blue t-shirt and levis is being pulled down 30th into the blaze of light by a big dog on a leash. Only when she jumps on the hood of the white police car behind the orange cord do I realize she's a cop too, the dog a Doberman. A white van is pulling up with some sort of ladder/tower on its roof. Suddenly the dark three at my Psyche take the formal shooting stance. *Ready. Aim . . . .* Suddenly a lot of men are running the alley behind 3021, one after another like wooden figures in a carnival shooting gallery. I dial Hunter again. Now they relax, pull back, the two across her front hood, the one at her back, just the barrel of his rifle over her left behind. In the play of shadows the dent beneath her left front headlight, from the night Patrick told me of his other lover, looks like the Black Hole of my soul. In fact, Psyche looks like all the other unloved vehicles on this street. I keep dialing, tilting the phone into the spotlights to find the holes. I can see the phone in the bus, ringing and ringing. Answer the phone Hunter. I can hear the phone ringing and ringing in Jimmy's house.

Jimmy you're gonna have to talk to me.

Jim. I want you to be a man.

Our laughter is a burst of gunshot onto the street. *Really, Jim. Be a MAN!*

Tree shadows dance the Indians' house. I wouldn't come out either. Cornered, I couldn't.

"He's probably paralyzed with fear," Starr whispers.

For me it would be pride. The despair of letting the assholes win again, the despair of going back to prison. I'm not leaving, Sitting Bull said to the Indian police. And so they mowed him down. Time can do so much. It seems like it's been hours, but I still can't take my eyes off the house. I can see Jimmy lying on the bathroom floor, spacing out on the cool tile.

"Maybe he's stoned. Doesn't quite get it," Starr says.

Maybe he's dead in the bathroom. Ran in there, swallowed every pill, lay down on the sweet floor, remembering Lloyd, how they killed him, how brief the time between your donut at 7-11 and the whole neighborhood firebombed. Remembering the SLA firebombed in Watts when you were a boy, and all the movies forever, your heart at Wounded Knee and Alcatraz, Spanish for pelican, that most graceful prehistoric creature flying endangered over the bay. Then the Indian occupation. Part of the controversy about firebombing the MOVE is how long they waited. Letting her burn over an hour before they sent in the fire trucks. Now the LA police chief wants the Philadelphia chief to run for President. He's my hero, he said. They'd never firebomb a white neighborhood, Starr says. How about a poor mixed one, like Southeast Portland? Belmont's the main drag for hooligans, but no, I don't get afraid here. I like it. $65 a month for this space. Telling her about Max, how I met him when he was doing time in LA County Jail. Refused to be drafted, then drugs. Once they got their hands on him. The LA police had it out for him. He was crazed. We moved to Vermont. Only thing that saved him, I think. And me and the kids.

She gets Dane on the phone. "Yeah, obviously. A dead man." In the side window of the house on our left I see the dark form of a woman huddled on the floor. Candles at her knees.

Jim. This is your Uncle Bob. Why don't you God damn it give it up?

"Dane says we should do something."

"We could get on that mike. Offer him a blowjob."

Our laughter's gonna get us a bullet between the eyes. When she's finished I dial the bus again. The phone rings in my ear, a dead grey buzzing and buzzing through the wrecks, the lonely high-pitched ringing across the street. Answer the phone, Hunter. *Please.*

"A friend just came back from Northern Ireland," Starr is saying now. "He said the police have roof towers on every block so that *every* house in the country is under twenty-four hour surveillance."

The house with its mouth agape. A child's doll house. Game house on Monopoly Avenue. Come out and play Jimmy Lee. People are gathered on the corner for you. There's a man now with a picket sign. CHOKED TO DEATH FOR THE COLOR OF HIS FLESH. A woman is carrying a little boy on her shoulders. Can you hear him calling you Jimmy? *La lo.* When your Mama had you, a baby boy, she knew this was the future, some version of this battle. He will kill or be killed.

We trade places beneath the window. Starr puts her head out a little into the night. "My mother was sixteen when I was born. My aunt describes seeing her hold me at the window, standing behind a curtain sobbing while I nursed. She was watching the high school kids come down the street."

"We're all emotional retards," I sigh to the long black braid down the back half-out the window. "You can't remember what you didn't experience consciously, but like a sponge you took that in."

Dialing again and again. The convolutions I start to go through. Resist. This is to be great love. Please oh please Hunter don't start playing games with me, don't get fucked up. Remember our first night vows. *To keep it holy.* Mama always told me you have to play hard to get. It's a man's nature to pursue. Otherwise he'll feel pursued. But I can't possibly play those games. Now a cop is running up the street. Suddenly spotlights from the far side of the Indian's house. They shine right through the top floor, right into Jimmy's. Now a light shining in my eyes from the roof of the Credit Union on Belmont. A loud jingling in the cop's pockets as he moves into shooting position behind the green and yellow Buick. *La lo,* the boy on his mother's neck sings. *Forget the entanglement of love.* But why didn't you tell me where you were going? I told you. Once you said it's important not to tell everything, but I *want* to tell you everything. Though it's *you* who keeps saying you can't trust *me*. Voices around the back of our house. A heavy scraping like a ladder being set up. Sharpshooter position on top of our roof. A new gun barrel sticking up over the back of Psyche.

"Glad I'm not inside her sleeping," I laugh. "Times I *have* been, with men leaning up against her sides, talking in the middle of the night, wondering about my white dog sitting there. No idea I'm inside. Last year we were sleeping down a steep incline from my kids' father's apartment in Manhattan Beach and someone icepicked the tires!"

Wednesday was our first fight. He blamed me for Moonlight's death. "You *deserted* him," he said of my leaving him at my brother's for two months while I went on the reading tour for my book. I could hear the fear that I'd desert him, but still, that he would blame me . . . .

A huge explosion over on Belmont. "Maybe it's to make Jimmy nervous. Psychological sound effects."

A lowered orange car comes tooling down 30th. Stops at the sight of all the cops. Then another *POP!* It backs up going 30-40 miles per hour. Staring at the house. Trying to pray. Dear Lord dear Jimmy Lee dear Hunter I used to pray as a girl. When I couldn't believe anymore I broke myself of the habit. Then the poems started. Another blast. *"Blast"* is the word I hear on the walky-talky atop Psyche. A huge book falls to the floor by my knees. *The Encyclopaedea of Women's Myths and Secrets.* Opened at *Aphrodisiac. Aphrodite.*

"You know," Starr says. "I have to tell you this. I told a mutual friend of Hunter's and mine about you. He said 'I wonder how long it'll be before he kicks her out like all the rest.'"

◇ ◇ ◇

Jim.

Jim. This is your Dad. You know we've been through this before. Why don't you give it up God damn it.

◇ ◇ ◇

Midnight. Hunter finally answers the phone. You won't believe what's happening. The words seem preposterous. He's naked on the other end.

"Lloyd Stevenson," he responds when I finally find them. "And the Philadelphia MOVE case might save Jimmy."

All the lights on the street go off. KEEP THE LIGHTS ON! a police radio blares. KEEP THE LIGHTS ON!

Another blast.

Jim.

This is your mother.

Holy Goddess, his mother!

They won't let me come in there and talk to you, Jimmy.

Her voice like a blues singer into the violent Northwestern night, like Joni singing after all these years I need your love. I crane out the window trying to see her.

"Can you hear her, honey?"

"Yeah. I can hear her."

The phone continues to ring and ring in the house. Say some more Mom. Don't stop now. Tell him you love him, you need his love. God speed his love.

Jim.

Her voice like pelicans flying free of Alcatraz. Her voice like a bell ringing sweetheart child, time to come home from playing, the sun is going down.

Jimmy, please. I'm sorry. They won't let me come in there to you.

Her voice, first voice ever heard, calling you out. It's been so long since we were able to talk Jimmy, since you became a man. I know how a boy has to leave his mother to become a man. My brothers when they came home from Viet Nam, they couldn't come home to our mother.

Jim! God damn it. This is your dad. They got about 500 people out here. You better God damn it come out!

"Fuck! Leave his mother on the phone! No way is he going to come out by threat."

The lights come back on. A tall blonde in levis is in the driver's seat of the Dodge.

"What would *you* say to the guy?" Hunter asks.

"I don't know. I'd just start talking. I'd talk and talk. I'd talk him into coming out, that's for sure. I wouldn't curse him."

"Well, pretend I'm Jimmy. Let me hear what you'd say."

I clam up. Carotid artery hold. "I couldn't possibly *pretend*. I could only do it if it was real."

"You can lay the phone down," he offers, helpfully. "I can hear the street noises."

"No! I want to share this with you.",

But really I'm on the basement floor with Jimmy. Elevation 77 feet. South and east of where the Columbia is entered by the Willamette and the two bank against the Tualatins. The Snake. The Clackamas. The Molalla. The Santiam. The Calapooia. The McKinzie. The Tualatin. First time here years ago, my plane from LA setting down on the Columbia, between Mount Hood and St. Helens before she blew her top, I couldn't believe how beautiful.

"Maybe you should go down to that microphone and talk to him yourselves. Two of the finest wordsmiths in the country right across the street, it seems it behooves you two to say something."

Yamhill looms expectantly. But I can't imagine getting to the green Dodge parked down there. The tall blonde wasn't his mother, just another cop.

"It's no man's land out there." God I'd do anything to win this man's respect.

"No woman's land," he corrects me with a little laugh, new to my feminism. Why do I feel I have to win his respect?

I hand the phone to Starr. Tell Uranus in the Tenth we should do something. She'll be able to start it. My Uranus will complete it. I stick my head out the window. Life in the Great Northwest Somewhere. Hunter watched St. Helens erupt from downtown. I can see that old guy Harry Truman refusing to be evacuated. I see that bus driver falling asleep at the wheel as we pull north up the coast of Peru, me and mi hija in the front seat, eighty folks behind us. How painful it was to overcome my hypnosis to wake him. Always I just want to go along for the ride.

"I think this is all your woman's fault," Starr is laughing. "She was just telling me in Mars how weird things always happen to her in Portland. She thinks there's an earth vortex under the city like the Gold Hill-Mt. Shasta Vortex."

"It's those two rivers," I sigh. "The Willamette pushes the Columbia *north* for Heaven's sake!" It's mountains on the *west*, weirdest of all, to me. It's some kind of Local Attraction, my inner compass doesn't work.

The phone continues to ring in the house. So much commotion, the tax payer's dollar, but really, there just isn't anyone home. Now I have to fight bursting into tears, Elvis crying from the corner *I'm so lonely I could die.* Starr telling my love who thinks I should go out there, both our men saying we should save the boy, about my hair in the police light. That dream I had last week, his face on a kite high in the sky, barely hanging onto him with my string. I'd read that article earlier that now instead of points they know the cell is made of strings. Women could have told them that a long time ago. In fact, we did. We got burned for it.

"The people in that house," Starr is chatting to Hunter, "maybe welfare. There's a young man who watches me from the porch. Seems fascinated by what I'm doing. Yes. It could be Jimmy. Whoever he is, I don't think he's seen many writers."

She hands the phone back to me. I can feel him shivering through the wires. I hold the phone while he gets some clothes on, my eyes glued to Jimmy's house. *Eros, I named my van Psyche to find you.* When he comes back I exclaim *Portland the only woman police chief in the country!*

"Is Penny Harrington a mother?" I ask then to either one.

Neither knows.

"She's *Ms Magazine's* Woman Of The Year," Starr says.

"If women had power everyone thinks it'd be just the same old story, just sexism reversed." I watch the woman cop below me adjust something on her belt. "As male-identified women like Penny Harrington show. But a society *organized* on women's values would be different." I'm trying not to shout it at her. I'm hanging out the window, talking too loud. I'm looking so far north I can see Richard Brautigan trout fishing as a boy on his Tacoma street, hear his mother calling him home years before he killed himself last winter.

"There'd be equality of the sexes and of the races and equality for the children as there was for 20,000 years in the ancient Mediterranean!" Now Hunter's telling me to get back in. "The central partnership would be mother and son, not the masculine imbalance, father and son!" "You're going to get your head blown off." A cop shines his flashlight up into my face. I see his before I duck. A Vietnamese cop.

I found him crying in the wrecks that second day, sobbing *I can't believe you've come to me. I feel so overwhelmed, so inadequate.* He says we'll heal ourselves in this love. He says it's our duty to the world. To show that love is possible.

But you can't remember what you didn't experience consciously, you can't change the unconscious until it becomes conscious. Sometimes at night I wake to all the wrecks starting up, hear and see the torn drivers grinding again in the chained melody of fire, metal, semen, heart. On the nightstand the cast bronze body parts of his old lovers, mostly nipples, but bellies, shoulders, and feet too. A lone gunman target practicing over the hill. I wake to my womb hysteria, his heart impotency, their dynamiting Earth into a gravel pit, all the dead sons wandering the foundry trying to get back home.

"Oh god, Starr, *look!*"

Two guys on the porch of the Indian house sneaking up on Jimmy's windows.

"Sharpshooters."

◇ ◇ ◇

"There he is there he is there he is!"

Whispering this into the phone.

A man in a white long-sleeved shirt, dark vest, levis. His hand on his silver belt buckle. The other swinging loosely, a little arrogantly, a lit cigarette in the fingers. He's large. I can't see the top of his head. He moves into the living room toward the door so nonchalantly, a man with plenty of time.

"Now he's disappeared."

"He's standing there behind the door," Starr whispers, nodding with her head.

"I don't see him."

Five minutes go by. The house just as before, the hours before. Quiet. He really was in there all that time. Amazing. A cowboy! But who were those punks? Jewelry, rhinestones, something on his chest.

"Here he comes again."

A very alone young man, circling. The kitchen, the living room, the bedroom, the hallway, the kitchen again. Into their lights and out again. Here I am. Don't shoot. When I step out that door.

I hold the phone out the window, not breathing, waiting for the massacre. Starr makes whimpering sounds.

He comes through the door onto the porch. Cowboy hat. Shiney boots. A large man with short blond curly hair. They swarm him from every direction, from under the house, their dark uniforms, their enormous guns. Starr moans. Time goes by so slowly. Bad Karma shoots across the street. He goes down to the ground in slow motion, face down, a free man, an endangered species, *caught*! They are handcuffing him for a long time. One pulls off his boots. Like the Pendleton Round-Up, tying the bull's feet. How often they've practiced this. Like watching a football game with the sound off. Now six from the street, one behind the other, storm the house. Now the one feels far up the leg. How good the dewy grass feels on your face. Being loved from behind second favorite position. As your mother goes deeper, dilating open. As they work over her to get you out, your grandfather who escaped jail dead on the surgeon's table at thirty-six.

After a very long time they have Jimmy up. Moving him to the waiting car. Silence.

The street is like the moment you died.

Suddenly Starr pushes past my shoulder, shouts at the top of her lungs, "YOU DID THE RIGHT THING, JUM. SURRENDER-IN."

She renders this statement in the identical voice, accent, inflections of the mother, father, girlfriend and uncle. An Eastern Oregon girl. *Ya did the ri-ight theng, Jum. Sur REN der'n.*

A man with a Doberman and wool cap emerges out from under us, from our own front porch as if in readiness for the riot to ensue from her yell.

Jimmy looks up just as he is being put in the backseat, his hands bound too tight behind him, all the cops around him like they've captured Big Foot. How I die now to speak my part. *We love you, Jim.* How he needs the words. But the Evil Spirit has me at the throat.

On the phone my love is laughing in celebration of Starr's declaration. Her voice cracked the whole street open.

The car speeds off. Jim in the backseat.

The orange cord at the end of the street is gone. My Psyche is not propping up shotguns.

"You'll be home after you dance?"

"Yeah."

Laughter.

◇ ◇ ◇

Down into the one a.m. street. Into the movie screen. The historic battlefield. Bad Karma dashes by me, up our stairs. TRUST JESUS graffitied on the asphalt. It's June one! Happy Birthday Marilyn Monroe, Allen Ginsberg.

I get caught in the man's face on the steps of the Command Center. Indian, Asian, the contours a field of boulders. Half Caucasian, maybe. Starr walks briskly up to him.

"I'm a reporter for *The Oregonian.*" Her and her Uranus.

"I don't know anything. I just live here."

He directs us to the U.S. Marshall standing on the corner under the undulating, meaty maple. A blaze of silver at two other reporters. Starr repeats her claim.

"What did the guy do?" I ask, getting a whiff of his after-shave.

"I don't know what he did." He's wearing a three-piece silver suit with a silver windbreaker over it. Gold lettering, *U.S. Marshall* across his left tit. "All I know is that he was doing time at Terminal Island. He was put on a train to report to a half-way house in Wyoming. He didn't show. In the federal system that constitutes *escape.* That's why we were called in."

The maple dips like an emotional woman to his silver head. Cops are so effeminate in their immaculate clothes, their shaved necks.

"We received information that he had a gun. So that's why we contacted the Portland Police."

"How old is he?"

"He's twenty five."

"Where's he from?"

"He was born in Madras."

"Why didn't he come out?"

Blank. Nothing. House with its mouth open.

"Look." He turns directly into my face. "I hope you give some credit to the Portland Police. They handled this very well." In the dead light of his eyes I see them beating Jimmy in the backseat on the way to the station. That boy long ago they busted on my beach for nudity, treated so gently in my presence. Later the boy came back, told me how they beat him unconscious the seven miles up the Coast Highway to the Mailbu jail.

"All these cops, gimme a break!" Starr introduces me to her landlord. "So Jimmy's a little macho? Being from Eastern Oregon I can recognize the syndrome." He and Starr laugh heartedly.

Now a guy my size is standing with us. Cowboy hat, moustache, young.

"This is Jimmy's brother," the landlord says. Jimmy's brother's eyes green like a desert flashflood into mine.

"Darlene don't know it," he says, dashing his cigarette to the lawn. "But she's to blame for all this."

"What do you mean?"

"Jimmy had all her money, three thousand bucks and had changed all the titles to his name. All these junk cars here on the street." His upper lip, heavily haired, flairs. "Well, they're engaged to be married, whud' she expect?" The proverbial shoulder shrug. *Love!* I keep from screaming. "She filed for lost titles. They ran a make, found out he was here." He lights up a cigarette. "Still ain't no reason to aim 500 guns at a guy's door."

Then Darlene is coming down the one a.m. street. Face wide like Libra, Aquarius maybe. Two moon slivers over her lostlake eyes.

"This is Jimmy Lee's fiance, Darlene," Jimmy's brother says. "Darlene, these are poets."

"Yeah?" She blows a kiss to the silver maple. "I'm a poet too." Then she spins around, two-stairs in her coyboys up her famous porch, back into the house still lit from inside. "And this poet's goin dancin."

"She's a poet and she knows it," the brother says.

It takes me a few seconds. "And I just hope we don't blow it." Then I ask him. "What was Jimmy doing in there all that time? Why didn't he come out?"

"If you could see that basement, you'd know. Piles and piles of women's clothes. All purple. Darlene's about to open The Purple Shop. Jimmy coulda stayed hid for a million years in them purple dresses." He drags on his cigarete. "He just needed time to think. Knowin Jim. A few cigarettes."

"I don't know about anyone else," Darlene hollers, bounding down her steps in a glittery purple western shirt, a white Stetson, "but *I'm* goin dancin."

"I'll go dancing with you Darlene," I holler back.

"I can't *believe* you're going dancing now," Starr says.

"You come too," I say to her black braid as she moves out into the night.

She's chuckling, moving across the street to her own porch. I look up to the crow's nest, the widow's walk, her room of her own where we are crouched for the siege.

"Ho!" Mona Lisa turns her face back to me. "No way *I'm* going dancin."

◇ ◇ ◇

I move down the sorrowing street to Psyche. A couple, dark and sullen, inside a dirty beat-up white stationwagon. I ♥ JACK in red on the bashed bumper. Door hanging open.

"Excuse me." They are just sitting here, staring into the night. I ♥ JACK on the front bumper too.

"Yeah, I'm his Dad. What kinda writer are you?"

"I'm a poet."

If I could describe this father bent over his crummy steering wheel, just staring into the Scorpio moon forty-four hours to full, an intensity, a knowledge about something he's always known, never been able to say, then I'd really be a poet.

"His crime? My oldest boy's stupid, that's all. Been stupid since he was twelve, thirteen. Oldest of my five sons. Stupid. Just stupid. But *not* violent. He never hurt nobody. His crime? You wanna know his crime?"

His irony would kneel a cop.

"Jimmy went up the Yellowstone, picked up some elk antlers. Which is illegal." He says *ee-lee-gawl*. "He served two-and-a-half years in the federal pen for that. Yellowstone's a *National* Park. Stupid, that's all. He has a history of not showin up. Just don't show. So why all the guns I'd like to know. Once they told him he had to appear in court. And he didn't. They busted him for two years for that. Now this. He didn't have no gun in there. Jimmy's stupid, but he never did nothin violent." If I could describe his face like a stupid jack rabbit run over on the interstate.

"It's gettin to be bad as Russia anymore. Youda thought he was a murderer."

I look down the woman's thin back, pitched forward to the dash. A red windbreaker with STP circled. He keeps saying *my son*. I hold back the question, "Is he your son, too?" If you birth a son there's a 30% greater chance your husband will stay.

"They told us," she says, staring into the black windshield, "we could talk to him when he come out. But they just drove on past. Like we was nothing."

"I wouldn't have come out either," I offer. Oh, I keep offering this. If there's any truth I know about this evening it's this one. Stupid, that's all.

"He was on his way to the half-way house, Wyoming, Montana, some place like that. Up from California . . ."

"No, Jack. The Terminal Island in Washington . . . ."

"And he just got off the train when it come through Portland. Come see Darlene, his fiance is all. The town he grew up in. Can hardly blame a guy." He looks up at me. "Been here two months."

"It was Easter, I remember, when he got here," the mother says.

Two months. That's me in Scorpio's Wrecking Yard. I probably shouldn't have come running back from Wyoming so fast when he asked, but I couldn't resist. To play games, pretend you don't love, a sacrilege. But sometimes at 2:20 am in the pouring down rain the train comes through waking me from a dream of climbing Mt. Hood. Sometimes I see Moonlight wandering the yard, pissing around the foundry, the girls stripping for the boys out on the highway at the Q.T. In the jet skylights I see my father falling through Bootes, listen to him sleep beside me, wishing he'd wake up, make love to me. "Well, if *you* were God," he said, first hostility in his voice, "how would *you* change things?" Then I know he *can't* come out, they've got him surrounded, they're out there now just waiting to pick him off, and it's *my* voice calling him out. When I asked what "story" means to him he said it's the Lone Ranger riding off into the sunset. Fight or flight, you motherfucker, love is an illness, the way she talked to you when you were two, we must all become more masculine. Jimmy's parents just sit here, staring into the street lamp. I'd start with father and child. I'd have the men raise the children. To alter the psyche of the human species. In the two year old's turning from the mother lies culture's turning from the feminine. The Man always seems freedom from the first God, the first tyrant.

The mother is still young, built very slight. "My brother Bob," she says from revery, "works for the police some. He really tried to help." Her son must be twice as big as she. He must have hurt a lot. Her long limp dark hair pulled onto her narrow back by a red rubberband. Five sons. She is so quiet. So still. Soon I will be dancing. I will follow Darlene's instructions out Southeast 82nd to King Road. What time do the bars close in Oregon anyway? Plenty of time she'll say, her ten long purple nails in Psyche's half-lowered window. But Jimmy's whole fuckin family's here now, I gotta talk to em. But wait for me darlin, I'll be there, I gotta dance. Her soft silver flesh, oh, yeah, Jimmy, jump off that train, slip on down, into town, into her bed, her purple dreams, forget Terminal Island. Next week she'll wrap the whole house in a purple ribbon, FREE JIMMY LEE! But now, no bullet holes in your Psyche, make it on out. To a dark street behind The Harmony. Park under an Oregon locust tree. So many Harleys. Remove your SUPPORT NICARAGUA button, don't get raped, run. Like you been here a thousand times. Like the lead singer is your friend. Like Moonlight's at your side. A hundred people dancing, drunk, so late, *really* drunk. They got their motorcycle jackets on too. They look. You look back. They look away. High Lonesome Blues. Bass player looks like someone you used to know, a writer about whales. No one's going to ask you here, this late. A woman dancing by herself, not here. Go pee instead. A blonde, six foot before the mirror, eye make-up like Bad Karma applying her blush, her arm so young over her head, the large loose breast, nipple sort of old under the pink shirt, oh you wanna you wanna you wanna dance. Lay your jacket over the fence in front of the band. Ask a very drunk long haired skinny biker shorter than you. Really. Yeah.

So you dance. Never could read or write. But he could play the guitar so good.

"If I coulda just talked to him. They wouldn't let me talk to him. They held me back from the loudspeaker. I kept begging them. I couldn't just *talk* to Jimmy, I had to be *escorted* every time by a Marshall. And only for that one time did they let me talk to my boy. They made me stay back."

After a while I say from my own revery. "Did he shoot the elk?"

"No!"

"NO! NO! NO!" The father's contempt would make a U.S. Marshall know birth. "You *know*."

I don't.

"Once a year elk shed their antlers. Jimmy just picked them up. That's his crime. That's right, darlin. You got it. They just rot on the ground otherwise. A pair of elk antlers weighs about fifteen pounds, you can get $50-$60 a pound for them. They send them over to Japan, you know, the velvet is an aphrodisiac."

"They told us we could talk to him when he come out," the mother says, still unmoving. Lanced into the windshield. "But they didn't let us. They speeded up when they saw us. They were lyin all along."

This story is dedicated to Timothy Baumel, age 14, killed by the Portland Police November 27, 1987.

Sharon Doubiago was born and raised in Southern California and has spent much of her adult life traveling the Americas. Her epic poem, *Hard Country*, was published in 1982 and a collection of stories, *The Book Of Seeing With One's Own Eyes*, in 1987. In 1989, along with *El Niño*, she will publish *South America Mi Hija*, a booklength narrative poem, and *Psyche Drives the Coast, Poems 1975-1987*. She considers the West Coast—San Diego to Seattle (Tijuana to Victoria)—her home.